HAUNTINGS

Ghosts and Ghouls from Around the World

Other books by Margaret Hodges:

Saint George and the Dragon
The Voice of the Great Bell
The Arrow and the Lamp: The Story of Psyche
Buried Moon

HAUNTINGS

Ghosts and Ghouls from Around the World

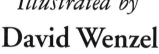

Compiled and retold by
Margaret Hodges

Illustrated by
David Wenzel

Little, Brown and Company
Boston   Toronto   London

First Edition

The characters and events portrayed in this book are fictitious. Any similarity to real persons, living or dead, is coincidental and not intended by the author.

Library of Congress Cataloging-in-Publication Data

Hauntings : ghosts and ghouls from around the world /
  compiled and retold by Margaret Hodges ; illustrated by David
  Wenzel. — 1st ed.
     p. cm.
  Summary: A collection of folktales from around the world
  featuring ghosts, witches, and monsters.
  ISBN 0-316-36796-6
  1. Tales [1. Folklore.] I. Hodges, Margaret, 1911–   . II.
Wenzel, David, 1950– ill.
  PZ8.1.C163 1991
  398.2 — dc20   90-27071

10 9 8 7 6 5 4 3 2 1

MV NY

Published simultaneously in Canada
by Little, Brown & Company (Canada) Limited

Printed in the United States of America

For our grandchildren with love from Grumma
— M. H.

Contents

❧

Preface

ও

Before we begin . . .

Can you hear their voices?

Some say that all the sounds since time began echo on forever and ever in outer space. If this is so, the myriad sounds of ordinary life must resound there — and also the crashing of monsters through primeval jungles. The rattle of bones. The eerie songs of night birds. The tolling of unseen bells. Gentle voices calling from the other side of the veil that separates the living and the dead. Voices pleading for mercy, screaming in fear. The tones a storyteller once used to make old and young laugh or cry.

Some say, "I have never heard those echoes. Therefore they do not exist." But others say, "What if we could invent a huge listening device to reach into outer space and bring back all the echoes of the past? Or maybe we only need open ears."

Those who have ears to hear, let them hear.

Acknowledgments

"Aunt Tildy's Ghost Story" retold from "A Ghost Story" in *Nights with Uncle Remus: Myths and Legends of the Old Plantation* by Joel Chandler Harris. Boston: J. R. Osgood, 1883.

"The City at the Bottom of the Sea" adapted from *The Wonderful Adventures of Nils* by Selma Lagerlof, translated by Velma S. Howard. New York: Doubleday, 1907.

"The Tinker and the Ghost" from *Three Golden Oranges and Other Spanish Folk Tales* by Ralph Steele Boggs and Mary Gould Davis, illustrated by Emma Brock. Copyright © 1936 by Longmans, Green and Co. Copyright renewed 1964 by Ralph Steele Boggs and Perley B. Davis. Reprinted by permission of David McKay Company, Inc.

"Godfather Death" retold from *Household Tales* by the Brothers Grimm, translated by Margaret Hunt. London: G. Bell, 1884.

"The Hungry Old Witch" from *Tales from Silver Lands* by Charles J. Finger, copyright © 1924 by Doubleday, a division of Bantam, Doubleday, Dell Publishing Group, Inc. Used by permission of the publisher.

"The Coffin Lid" retold from *Russian Folk Tales* by W. R. S. Ralston. London: Smith, Elder and Company, 1873.

"The Stone Boat" adapted from "The Stone Boat" in *Wander Ships* by Wilbur Bassett. Chicago: Open Court Publishing Company, 1917.

"Tiny Man" retold from "Tiddy Mun," collected by Marie Clothilde Balfour in "Legends of the Cars," *Folk-Lore,* vol. II, no. II (June 1891).

"The Bells of Ys" slightly adapted from *The Other World: Myths of the Celts* retold by Margaret Hodges. New York: Farrar, Straus & Giroux, 1973.

"The Haunted Harp" adapted from the old ballad "Binnorie."

"The Golem" retold from *Miracles of the Maharal* (17th century) as found in *A Treasury of Jewish Folklore,* Nathan Ausubel, ed. New York: Crown, 1948.

"Lord of the Dead" retold from "Savitri's Choice," an adaptation from the *Mahabharata* in *From Umar's Pack,* compiled and edited by Effie Power. New York: Dutton, 1937.

↶ Acknowledgments ↷

"Snow" from *Kwaidan: Stories and Studies of Strange Things* by Lafcadio Hearn. Boston: Houghton, Mifflin and Company, 1904.

"The Kindly Ghost" retold from *A Book of Ghosts and Goblins* by Ruth Manning Sanders. London: Methuen, 1968.

"The Bunyip" retold from *The Brown Fairy Book* by Andrew Lang. New York: Longmans, 1904.

"Joe Magarac, Steel Man" with acknowledgment to George Carver's "Legend of Steel," *Western Pennsylvania Historical Magazine* 27, nos. 3–4 (1944): 132–36.

HAUNTINGS

Ghosts and Ghouls from Around the World

Aunt Tildy's Ghost Story

We are in Uncle Remus's cabin on a Georgia plantation before the Civil War, but this time Uncle Remus isn't sharing stories about Brer Rabbit. His friend Aunt Tildy knows a good tale about a haunt, and she tells it — for revenge.

ɕ୨

Aunt Tildy was angry with Daddy Jack because he had said she was pigeon-toed, but the next time the little boy, Joel, visited Uncle Remus he persuaded Tildy to go with him. Daddy Jack was in his usual place, dozing and talking to himself, while Uncle Remus oiled the carriage harness.

The conversation turned on stories about haunts and spirits, and finally Tildy spoke. "When it comes to tales about haunts," said she, "I heard one that'll just naturally make your hair stand on end. Uncle Remus, shall I tell it?"

"Let her come," said Uncle Remus.

"Well, then," said Tildy, "one time there was a Woman and a Man. Seemed like they lived close to one another, and the Man, he set his eyes on the Woman, and the Woman, she just went along and tended to her business. Man, he kept his eyes set on her. By and by, the Woman, she tended to her business so much that she took sick and died. Man, he up and tells the folks she's dead, and the folks they come in and fix her. They laid her out and they lighted some candles, and they sat up with her, just like folks do now; and they put two great big round shiny silver dollars on her eyes to hold her eyelids down."

To describe the silver dollars, Tildy joined the ends of her thumbs and forefingers together and made a figure as large as a saucer.

"They were lots bigger than dollars are in these days," she continued, "and they looked mighty pretty. Seemed like they were all the money the Woman had, and the folks put them on her eyelids to hold them down. Then when the folks did that they called the Man and told him that he must dig a grave and bury the Woman, and then they all went off about their business.

"Well, then, the Man, he took and dug the grave and made ready to bury the Woman. He looked at that money on her eyelids, and it shone mighty pretty. Then he took it off and felt it. It felt mighty good, but just about that time the Man looked at the Woman, and he saw her eyelids open. Looked like she was looking at him, and he took and put the money back where he got it from.

"Well, then, the Man, he took and got a wagon and hauled the Woman out to the burying ground, and when he got there he fixed everything, and then he grabbed the money and covered up the grave right quick. Then he went home, and he put the money in a tin box and rattled it around. It rattled loud and it rattled nice, but the Man, he wasn't feeling so good. Seemed like he knew the Woman's eyelids were stretched wide open looking for him. Yet he rattled the money around, and it rattled loud and it rattled nice.

"Well, then, the Man, he took and put the tin box with the money in it on the mantelshelf. The day went by, and the night came, and when the night came, the wind began to rise up and blow. It rose high, it blew strong. It blew on the top of the house, it blew under the house, it blew around the house. The Man, he felt queer. He sat by the fire and listened. Wind said, '*Buzz-zoo-o-o-o-o!*' Man listened. Wind hollered and cried. It blew on top of the house, it blew under the house, it blew around the house, it blew in the house. Man got close up to the fire. Wind found the cracks and blew in them. *Bizzy, bizzy, buzz-zoo-o-o-o-o!*

"Well, then, Man, he listened, listened, but by and by he got tired of this, and he said to himself that he was going to bed. He took and flung a fresh piece of wood in the fire, and then he jumped in the bed and curled himself up and put his head under the cover. Wind hunted for the cracks: *Bizzy-buzz, bizzy-buzz, buzz-zoo-o-o-o-o-o!* Man kept his head under the cover. The lighted knot of wood flared up and flickered. Man didn't dare to move. Wind blew and whistled,

Phew-fee-e-e-e! Lighted knot flickered and flared. Man, he kept his head covered.

"Well, then, Man lay there, and got scareder and scareder. He didn't dare to wink his eye scarcely, and it seemed like he was going to have swamp ague. While he lay there shaking, and the wind blowing, and the fire flickering, he heard some other kind of fuss. It was a mighty curious kind of fuss. *Clinkity, clinkalinkle!* Man said, 'Hey! Who's stealing my money?'

"Yet he kept his head covered while he lay and listened. He heard the wind blow, and then he heard that other kind of fuss: *Clinkity, clink, clinkity, clinkalinkle!* Well, then, he flung off the cover and sat right up in the bed. He looked; he didn't see nothing. The fire flickered and flared, and the wind blew. Man went and put the chain and bar across the door. Then he went back to bed, and he hadn't more than touched his head on the pillow when he heard the other fuss: *Clink, clink, clinkity, clinkalinkle!* Man rose up and didn't see nothing at all. Mighty queer!

"Just about the time he was going to lie down again, here came the fuss: *Clinkity, clinkalinkle.* It sounded like it was on the mantelshelf; not only that, it sounded like it was the money in the tin box on the mantelshelf. Man said, 'Hey! A rat's got in the box!'

"Man looked; no rat there. He shut up the box and set it down on the shelf. Soon as he did that, here came the fuss: *Clinkity, clinkity, clinkalinkle!* Man opened the box and looked at the money. Those two silver dollars were lying in there just like he put them. While the man did this, it looked like he could hear something say way off yonder, 'Where's my money? Oh, give me my money!'

"Man set the box back on the shelf, and as soon as he put it down, he heard the money rattle: *Clinkity, clinkalinkle, clink!* And then from way off yonder something said, 'Oh, give me my money! I want my money!'

"Well, then, the Man got scared sure enough, and he got a flatiron and put it on the tin box, and then he took and piled all the chairs against the door and ran and jumped into the bed. He just knew there was a booger coming. As soon as he got in bed and covered his head, the money rattled louder, and something cried way off yonder, 'I want my money! Oh, give me my money!'

"Man, he shook and he shivered; money, it clinked and rattled; booger, it hollered and cried. Booger came closer; money clinked louder. Man shook worse and worse. Money said, *'Clinkity, clinkalinkle!'* Booger cried, *'Oh, give me my money!'* Man hollered, *'O Lordy, Lordy!'*

"Well, then, it kept on this way, till all at once Man heard the door open. He peeped from under the cover, and in walked the Woman that he had buried in the burying ground. Man shivered and shivered, wind blew and blew, money rattled and rattled, Woman cried and cried. *'Buzz-zoo-o-o-o-o!'* said the wind. *'Clinkalink!'* said the box. *'Oh, give me my money!'* said the Woman.

'*O Lordy!*' said the Man. Woman heard the money, but it looked like she couldn't see, and she groped around, and groped around, and groped around with her hands raised in the air just this way."

Here Tildy stood up, pushed her chair back with her foot, raised her arms over her head, and leaned forward in the direction of Daddy Jack.

"Wind blew, fire flickered, money rattled, Man shook and shivered, Woman groped around and said, '*Give me my money! Oh, who's got my money?*'

Tildy advanced a few steps.

"Money looked like it was going to tear the tin box all to flinders. Woman groped and cried, groped and cried, till suddenly she jumped on the Man and hollered, '*You've got my money!*' "

Tildy sprang at Daddy Jack and seized him, and for a few minutes there was considerable confusion in the corner. Joel was frightened, but the collapsed appearance of Daddy Jack convulsed him with laughter. The old African was very angry, and he shook his cane threateningly at Tildy. She coolly adjusted her earrings, as she exclaimed, "There, now! I knew I'd get even with the old villain. Calling me pigeon-toed!"

The City at the Bottom
of the Sea

Ghosts from times long gone can reappear
on Easter Eve, marvelous and strange, full of
wildness and longing. In this tale from Sweden, it is the night of a full moon, too, which
gives Nils a chance that comes only one night
in every hundred years.

౿ఎ

*O*ne summer in Sweden, Nils Holgersson had a
wonderful adventure. He was transformed into an elf
and traveled with the wild geese all over his native
land.

One night they came to an island in the Baltic Sea.
It was a calm and clear night. The wild geese stood and
slept on a mountaintop, and the boy lay down in the
short, dry grass beside the geese. The moon was bright
that night, so bright that it was difficult for Nils to go
to sleep. He lay there wondering how long he had been
away from home. At the same time he remembered
that this was Easter Eve.

As the boy lay there with his nose in the air, thinking
about this, he caught sight of something lovely! The
moon's disc was whole and round and rather high, and
over it a big bird came flying. It did not fly past the

moon but seemed to be flying out from it. The body was small, the neck long and slender; the legs hung down, long and thin. It couldn't be anything but a stork.

A moment later the stork alit beside the boy. The bird bent down and poked Nils with his bill.

Instantly Nils sat up. "I'm not asleep," he said.

They chatted about all sorts of things, like old friends. At last the stork asked Nils if he wouldn't like to go out riding for a while on this beautiful night.

Oh, yes, he wanted to do it — if the stork would get him back to the wild geese before sunrise. This the stork promised, so off they went.

They flew straight toward the moon. They rose higher and higher. The sea was far below them. The flight went so light and easy that to Nils it seemed as if he were lying still in the air.

They landed on a desolate bit of seashore that was covered with fine, soft sand. All along the coast lay a row of sand dunes. The stork stood on a dune, drew up one leg, and bent his head backward, so that he could tuck his bill under his wing.

"You can roam around on the shore for a while," he said to Nils. "I will rest myself. Don't go so far away that you can't find your way back to me."

To start with, the boy intended to climb a sand dune to see what was behind it. But when he had gone a couple of steps, the toe of his wooden shoe touched something hard. He stooped down and saw a small copper coin lying on the sand. The coin was so old that it had turned green, and it was worth so little that Nils didn't even bother to pick it up but only kicked it out of the way.

When he straightened up, he was perfectly astounded, for two paces away from him stood a high, dark wall with a big, turreted gate. A moment before, only the sea had been there, shimmering and smooth. Now it was hidden by the long wall with towers and battlements. Directly in front of him, where there had been only a few seaweed banks, the big gate of the wall opened.

Both the wall and the gate were so beautifully constructed that Nils longed to see what might be behind them. *I must find out what this is,* he thought, and he went in through the gate.

In the deep archway were guards, dressed in brocaded and puffed suits, their long-handled spears beside them. They took no notice of the boy who hurried past them.

Just within the gate, Nils found an open space, paved with large, smooth stones. Round about were rows of high, magnificent buildings with long, narrow streets between them. The square swarmed with human beings. They wore plumed hats, and rich, golden chains hung against their chests. They might all have been kings.

The women, too, were beautifully dressed. They went about wearing high headdresses and long robes with tight-fitting sleeves. The boy simply couldn't believe his eyes.

But even more wonderful than the men and women was the city itself. Every house was built with a gable facing the street and was covered with the most handsome decorations.

As the boy was admiring all this, a sudden sense of haste came over him. *My eyes have never seen anything like this,* he said to himself. *Nothing like this will they ever see again.* He ran through the city, up one street, down another, wondering if it was all a dream.

The streets were full of people everywhere. Old women sat by their open doors, spinning. The merchants' shops opened onto the street, and all the craftsmen did their work out of doors. If only Nils had had time enough, he could have learned how to make all sorts of things. He saw armorers hammering out thin breastplates, jewelers setting precious stones in rings and bracelets, weavers weaving silver and gold threads into their cloth.

When he had run from one end of the city to the other, he came to a gate beyond which lay the sea and harbor. He saw ships of the olden time, taking on cargo or casting anchor. All was life and bustle.

The boy had run for so long that he was hot and tired. The street into which he turned next seemed to be where the people purchased the fabrics for their fine clothing. He saw crowds standing before the little stalls where merchants displayed brocades, stiff satins, heavy gold cloth, shimmery velvet, and laces as sheer as a spider's web.

Before, while he had been running, no one had paid any attention to him. But now, as he walked down the street, one of the salesmen caught sight of him and beckoned to him, spreading out on the counter a lovely piece of satin damask.

Nils shook his head. *I will never be so rich that I can buy even a yard of that cloth,* he thought.

By this time, the salesmen all along the street had caught sight of him. Wherever he looked, a salesman stood, beckoning to him. They fetched the best cloths they had to sell, and their hands trembled with eagerness and haste as they laid them on the counters.

When the boy kept on going, one of the merchants jumped over the counter, caught hold of him, and spread before him silver cloth and woven tapestries that shone in brilliant colors.

Nils could only laugh at him. The salesman must surely understand that a poor boy like him couldn't buy such things. He stood still and held out his two empty hands to show that he had nothing.

The merchant brought out a tiny, worn, and almost worthless coin and showed it to Nils. He was so eager to sell that he increased his pile with a pair of large, heavy silver goblets.

Then the boy began to dig down in his pockets. He knew, of course, that he didn't possess a single coin, but he couldn't help feeling for one.

When the other merchants saw the boy searching in his pockets, they took up handfuls of gold and silver ornaments and offered them to him. And they all showed him that what they asked in payment was just one little penny.

The boy turned both vest and breeches pockets inside out so that they should see he owned nothing. These merchants, who were so much richer than he, looked so distressed he wondered if he could not help them in some way. Then he happened to think of the tarnished coin that he had seen on the sand.

He started to run down the street, and luck was with him. He came to the same gate that he had happened upon at first. He dashed through it and commenced to search for the little green copper penny he had seen on the beach a while ago.

He found it, too, very promptly. But when he picked it up and started to run back to the city with it — he saw only the sea before him. No city walls, no gate, no sentinels, no streets, no houses — only the sea.

The boy couldn't help it that tears came to his eyes. He had believed, in the beginning, that what he had seen was only a dream, but he had already forgotten this. He only thought how beautiful it had been.

At that moment the stork awoke and came up to him. He had to poke Nils with his bill to attract attention to himself. "You must be able to sleep standing up the way I do," the stork said.

"What was that city that stood here just now?" the boy exclaimed.

"Have you seen a city?" asked the stork. "You must have slept and dreamed."

"No! I was not dreaming," said Nils, and he told the stork all that had happened.

Then the stork said, "I have heard that there was once a city on this shore, called Vineta. It was so rich and so fortunate that no city has ever been more glorious. But its people were too proud and loved only the things that money can buy. As a punishment, they say, Vineta was overtaken by a flood, and it sank into the sea. But these people cannot die, nor is their city destroyed. And one night in every hundred years, it rises in all its splendor up from the sea, for just one hour."

"Yes, it must be true," said Nils, "for I have seen it."

"But when the hour is up," said the stork, "if during that time no merchant in the city has sold anything to a single living creature, then Vineta sinks again into the sea. If you had had only a penny to pay the merchants, Vineta might have remained up here on the shore, and its people could have lived and died like other human beings."

"Now I understand why you came and fetched me in the middle of the night," said the boy. "It was because you believed that I might be able to save the old city. I am so sorry it didn't turn out as you wished."

It was hard to tell which one looked more disappointed, the boy or the stork. But where Vineta rose from the sea before the astonished eyes of Nils, there stands today the ruined city of Visby, "the city of ruins and roses." In the days of its glory it looked as Vineta looked to Nils.

The Tinker and the Ghost

On Halloween a certain haunted castle in
Spain is especially dangerous. Death awaits
anyone foolish enough to spend that night in
the castle. On the other hand, the rewards
are great for the one who can exorcise the
ghost.

か

*O*n the wide plain not far from the city of Toledo,
there once stood a great gray castle. For many years
before this story begins, no one had dwelt there, because the castle was haunted. There was no living soul
within its walls, and yet at night, a thin, sad voice
moaned and wept and wailed through the huge, empty
rooms. And on All Hallows' Eve, a ghostly light appeared in the chimney, a light that flared and died and
flared again against the dark sky.

Learned doctors and brave adventurers had come to
the castle on All Hallows' Eve and tried to exorcise the
ghost. Each one had been found the next morning in
the great hall of the castle, sitting lifeless before the
empty fireplace.

Now one day in late October there came to the little
village that nestled around the castle walls a brave and
jolly tinker whose name was Esteban. And while he sat

in the marketplace, mending the pots and pans, the good wives told him about the haunted castle. It was All Hallows' Eve, they said, and if he would wait until nightfall he could see the strange, ghostly light flare up from the chimney. He might, if he dared go near enough, hear the thin, sad voice echo through the silent rooms.

"If I dare!" Esteban repeated scornfully. "You must know, good wives, that I — Esteban — fear nothing, neither ghost nor human. I will gladly sleep in the castle tonight and keep this dismal spirit company."

The good wives looked at him in amazement. Did Esteban know that if he succeeded in banishing the ghost the owner of the castle would give him a thousand gold *reales?*

Esteban chuckled. If that was how matters stood, he would certainly go to the castle at nightfall and do his best to get rid of the thing that haunted it. But he was a man who liked plenty to eat and drink and a fire to keep him company. They must bring to him a load of fagots, a side of bacon, a flask of wine, a dozen fresh eggs, and a frying pan. This the good wives gladly did. And as the dusk fell, Esteban loaded these things onto his donkey's back and set out for the castle. And you may be very sure that not one of the village people went very far along the way with him!

It was a dark night with a chill wind blowing and a hint of rain in the air. Esteban unsaddled his donkey and set him to graze on the short grass of the deserted courtyard. Then he carried his food and his fagots into the great hall. It was dark as pitch there. Bats beat their soft wings in his face, and the air felt cold and musty. He lost no time in piling some of his fagots in one corner of the huge stone fireplace and in lighting them. As the red and golden flames leaped up the chimney, Esteban rubbed his hands. Then he settled himself comfortably on the hearth.

"*That* is the thing to keep off both cold and fear," he said.

Carefully slicing some bacon, he laid it in the pan and set it over the flames. How good it smelled! And how cheerful the sound of its crisp sizzling!

He had just lifted his flask to take a deep drink of the good wine when down the chimney there came a voice — a thin, sad voice. "*Oh, me!*" it wailed. "*Oh, me! Oh, me!*"

Esteban swallowed the wine and set the flask carefully down beside him.

"Not a very cheerful greeting, my friend," he said, as he moved the bacon on the pan so that it should be equally brown in all its parts. "But bearable to a man who is used to the braying of his donkey."

"*Oh, me!*" sobbed the voice. "*Oh, me! Oh, me!*"

Esteban lifted the bacon carefully from the hot fat and laid it on a bit of brown paper to drain. Then he broke an egg into the frying pan. As he gently shook the pan so that the edges of his egg should be crisp and brown and the yolk soft, the voice came again. Only this time it was shrill and frightened.

"*Look out below,*" it called. "*I'm falling!*"

"All right," answered Esteban, "only don't fall into the frying pan."

With that there was a thump, and there on the hearth lay a man's leg! It was a good enough leg, and it was clothed in half of a pair of brown corduroy trousers.

Esteban ate his egg and a piece of bacon and drank again from the flask of wine. The wind howled around the castle, and the rain beat against the windows.

Then, *"Look out below,"* called the voice sharply. *"I'm falling!"*

There was a thump, and on the hearth there lay a second leg, just like the first!

Esteban moved it away from the fire and piled on more fagots. Then he warmed the fat in the frying pan and broke into it a second egg.

"Look out below!" roared the voice. And now it was no longer thin, but strong and lusty. *"Look out below! I'm falling!"*

"Fall away," Esteban answered cheerfully. "Only don't spill my egg."

There was a thump, heavier than the first two, and on the hearth there lay a trunk. It was clothed in a blue shirt and a brown corduroy coat.

Esteban was eating his third egg and the last of the cooked bacon when the voice called again, and down fell first one arm and then the other.

Now, thought Esteban, as he put the frying pan on the fire and began to cook more bacon. *Now there is only the head left to fall. I confess that I am rather curious to see the head.*

"LOOK OUT BELOW!" thundered the voice. "I'M FALLING — FALLING!"

And down the chimney there came tumbling a head!

It was a good enough head, with thick black hair, a long black beard, and dark eyes that looked a little strained and anxious. Esteban's bacon was only half cooked. Nevertheless, he removed the pan from the fire and laid it on the hearth. And it is a good thing that he did, because before his eyes the parts of the body joined together, and a living man — or his ghost — stood before him! And *that* was a sight that might have startled Esteban into burning his fingers with the bacon fat.

"Good evening," said Esteban. "Will you have an egg and a bit of bacon?"

"No, I want no food," the ghost answered. "But I will tell you this, right here and now. You are the only man, out of all those who have come to the castle, to stay here until I could get my body together again. The others died of sheer fright before I was half finished."

"That is because they did not have sense enough to bring food and fire with them," Esteban replied coolly. And he turned back to his frying pan.

"Wait a minute!" pleaded the ghost. "If you will help me a bit more, you will save my soul and get me into the kingdom of heaven. Out in the courtyard, under a cypress tree, there are buried three bags — one of copper coins, one of silver coins, and one of gold coins. I stole them from some thieves and brought them here to the castle to hide. No sooner did I have them buried than the thieves overtook me, murdered me, and cut my body into pieces. But they did not find the coins. Now you come with me and dig them up. Give the copper coins to the church, the silver coins to the poor, and keep the gold coins for yourself. Then I will have expiated my sins and can go to the kingdom of heaven."

This suited Esteban. So he went out into the courtyard with the ghost. And you should have heard how the donkey brayed when he saw them!

When they reached the cypress tree in a corner of the courtyard, the ghost said, "Dig."

"Dig yourself," answered Esteban.

So the ghost dug, and after a time the three bags of money appeared.

"Now will you promise to do just what I asked you to do?" said the ghost.

"Yes, I promise," Esteban answered.

"Then," said the ghost, "strip my garments from me."

This Esteban did, and instantly the ghost disappeared, leaving his clothes lying there on the short grass of the courtyard. It went straight up to heaven and knocked on the gate. Saint Peter opened it and, when the spirit explained that he had expiated his sins, gave him a cordial welcome.

Esteban carried the coins into the great hall of the castle, fried and ate another egg, and then went peacefully to sleep before the fire.

The next morning when the village people came to

carry away Esteban's body, they found him making an omelet out of the last of the fresh eggs.

"Are you alive?" they gasped.

"I am," Esteban answered. "And the food and the fagots lasted through the night very nicely. Now I will go to the owner of the castle and collect my thousand gold *reales*. The ghost has gone for good and all. You will find his clothes lying out in the courtyard."

And before their astonished eyes he loaded the bags of coins on the donkey's back and departed.

First he collected the thousand gold *reales* from the grateful lord of the castle. Then he returned to Toledo, gave the copper coins to his parish priest, and faithfully distributed the silver ones among the poor. And on the thousand *reales* and the golden coins he lived in idleness and a great contentment for many years.

Godfather Death

Death confers weird powers on a doctor,
until he takes undue advantage of his gift and
finds that Death will always have the last
word. A story from the Germany of the
Brothers Grimm.

৩

$\mathcal{A}$ poor man had twelve children and was forced to
work night and day to give them even bread to eat.
When the thirteenth child was born, he ran out into
the highway, resolved to ask the first person he met to
be the child's godfather.

The first to meet him was God, who already knew
what filled his heart and said to him, "Poor man, I pity
you. I will hold your child at its christening and take
care of it and make it happy on earth."

The man said, "Who are you?"

"I am God."

"Then I don't want you for my child's godfather,"
said the man. "You give to the rich and leave the poor
to be hungry." He turned away from God and went on
down the road.

Then the Devil came to him and said, "What are you
looking for? Take me as a godfather for your child and
I will give him plenty of gold and all the joys of the
world as well."

The man asked, "Who are you?"

"I am the Devil."

"Then I don't want you for my child's godfather," said the man. "You deceive people and lead them astray."

The man went on until Death came striding up to him with withered legs and said, "Take me as godfather for your child."

The man asked, "Who are you?"

"I am Death, and I treat everyone equally."

Then said the man, "You are the right one. You take the rich as well as the poor. You shall be my child's godfather."

Death answered, "I will make your child rich and famous, for he who has me for a friend can lack nothing."

The man said, "Next Sunday is the christening. Be there at the right time." Death appeared as he had promised and stood as godfather in quite the usual way.

When the boy had grown up, his godfather one day appeared and said, "Come with me."

Death led the boy into a forest and showed him an herb that grew there. "As your godfather," Death said, "I should give you a present. I will make you a famous doctor. When you are called to a patient, I will always be there, and you will see me. If I stand by the head of the sick man, you may say with confidence that you will make him well again. Give him this herb, and he will recover. But if I stand by the patient's feet, he is mine, and you must say that no doctor in the world can save him. Only beware of using the herb against my will, or you may be in trouble."

It was not long before the youth was the most famous doctor in the whole world. People said, "He has only to look at a patient, and he knows at once whether he will recover or die." From far and wide people came to him and gave him so much money that he soon became a rich man.

Now it happened that the king became ill, and the doctor was called to say whether he could get well. But when the doctor came to the bed, Death was standing by the feet of the sick man, and no herb on earth could save him.

If I cheat Death, thought the doctor, *he will not like it, but since I am his godson, he will wink at it. I will risk it.* So he picked up the sick man and laid him the other way, so that now Death was standing by his head. Then the doctor gave the king some of the herb, and he recovered and was healthy again.

But Death came to the doctor, looking very angry. He shook his finger at him and said, "You have cheated me. This time I will pardon you because you are my godson. But if you try it again, it will cost you your neck, for I will take you away with me."

Soon afterward the king's daughter became very ill. She was his only child, and he wept day and night. He sent word that whoever rescued her from death should be her husband and inherit the crown. When the doctor came to the sick girl's bed, he saw Death by her feet. He ought to have remembered the warning given by his godfather, but he fell so deeply in love with the princess, because of her great beauty and his hope of being her husband, that he thought of nothing else. He did not see that Death was casting angry looks at him and shaking his fist. The doctor lifted the sick princess and placed her head where her feet had lain. Then he gave her some of the herb, and instantly her cheeks became rosy and she sat up, as well as ever.

When Death saw that he was cheated for a second time, he strode up to the doctor and said, "All is over with you. It is your turn." He seized him so firmly with his ice-cold hand that the doctor could not resist. Death led him to a cave below the earth. There he saw thousands and thousands of candles burning in countless rows, some large, some half-size, others small. Every instant some were extinguished and others were lit, so that the flames leaped hither and thither, always changing.

"See," said Death, "these are the lights of people's lives. The tall ones belong to children, the half-size ones to middle-aged people, and the short ones to old people. But sometimes children and young folks have only a short candle."

"Show me my candle," said the doctor, and he thought that it would be a tall one. But Death pointed to a short candle stub whose flame was almost out.

"There it is," he said.

"Ah, dear godfather," said the horrified doctor, "light a new one for me. Do it because you love me, so that I may enjoy my life and be king and marry the king's beautiful daughter."

"I cannot," answered Death. "One candle must go out before another one is lighted."

"Then light a new one from my candle so that the old flame will light the new one."

Death seemed about to do as the doctor asked. He took hold of a tall new candle in one hand and took the old, flickering candle stub in the other hand. But then, as if on purpose, as if to have his revenge, his fingers fumbled, and the candle stub fell and its light went out. The doctor fell to the ground and into the hands of Death.

The Hungry Old Witch

A primeval forest is haunted by a wicked witch who works spells and mixes poisons. With nightmarish power, she gives chase to her victims, a South American Hansel and Gretel.

ೞ

There once was a witch who was very old and always hungry. She lived long ago near a forest in Uruguay, where Brazil and Argentina touch. Those were the days when mighty beasts moved in the marshes and strange creatures with wings like bats flew in the air. There were also great worms then, so strong that they bored through mountains and rocks.

The old witch once caught one of the giant worms and killed it for the sake of the stone in its head. The stone was green and shaped like a blunt arrowhead, and whoever owned it could fly through the air between sunrise and sunset, but never in the night.

The old witch had another secret power. She knew how to make a powder from the fried bodies of tree frogs mixed with goat's milk. A sprinkling of this powder could make things grow in strange ways. With it the witch could turn plants into animals, vines into serpents, thornbushes into foxes, or little leaves into ants.

This old witch had lived for hundreds of years, devouring cattle and pigs and goats, sometimes carrying off in one night all the animals of a village. So men would put half of what they had into a corral outside the village, hoping that the old witch would take it and leave them in peace.

At last, in one village a brave boy refused to take animals to the corral when the time came for the old witch to visit there. He had had a dream in which he was a bird in a cage. A climbing vine with a white flower grew up and twisted its way between the bars. Then it changed into a smiling young girl who gave him a golden key. He unlocked the door of the cage and went away with the girl. He had not seen the end of the dream but had wakened with the sound of singing and music in his ears.

This dream gave the boy courage to look for the witch and put an end to her evil work, for he said, "It is not right to give her what we have grown and tended and to let her destroy us."

Hearing this, the wise men of the village called him Stout Heart. But because they loved him, they trembled and turned pale when he took his lance and went off into the forest.

Stout Heart walked for three days before he at last sat down to rest under a tree by the side of a lake. Tired out, he tried to sleep, but he dreamed of harmful things that seemed to come out of the ground. So he climbed into the tree and found a place to rest among the branches.

While he slept, the old witch came to the side of the lake. She threw a net into the water and began to catch fish, singing in a croaking voice a charm that made things come to her. She filled her net again and again and threw the fish into wicker cages.

When he heard the singing, Stout Heart woke up and saw the wrinkled crone with her great pile of fish. He was sorry for such a waste of good life and regretted that he had left his spear hidden in the grass. He was weak from hunger and thirst, so he sat very still.

But the witch saw the tree and the boy reflected in the lake, and she looked up, straight at him. She did not have her magic green stone with her, and she could not climb trees, so she said, "You are faint and hungry. Come down, come down, good lad, for I have plenty of good things to eat."

Stout Heart only laughed and said he would stay where he was. So she spread fruits and berries on the grass and said in a wheedling voice, "Come, my boy, eat with me. I am very lonesome, and I want to treat you like a son."

Stout Heart was hungrier than ever, but he only said, "Have you any more traps to set for me?"

The old witch fell into a black and terrible rage, dancing about and gnashing her teeth, frothing at the mouth and hooking her long nails at him like a cat, but even though the boy saw her great strength, he didn't lose heart. He stayed in the tree.

In her great rage she picked up a rock the size of a

man's body and threw it at the tree so hard that the tree shook from root to tip. Then down she went on her hands and knees and made a little heap of grass blades, all the time cursing and groaning, grumbling and snarling like a cat. She sprinkled a gray powder over the grass heap, mumbling, "Creep and crawl, creep and crawl. Make him drop like rotting fruit!"

Presently the pile of grass began to move, and the grass blades became smaller. They turned round and brown. Then hairlike points shot out and became the legs of ants. Up the tree trunk the ants scurried and swarmed, marching over every leaf and twig until the green tree turned brown. The nearer to Stout Heart they came, the louder the old witch shrieked, leaping about and waving her long-taloned hands.

Stout Heart knew he could not fight so many ants. He climbed higher and higher in the tree, crawling along a branch that hung over the lake. But nearer and nearer the ants came until they were swarming over his hands and running up his arms. He let go and went with a splash into the green-blue water of the lake.

Suddenly he found himself in the old witch's net, being drawn to shore. He struggled and tried to escape, but it was of no use. He was all mixed up with other lake things — with fish and scum, with water beetles and sticky weed, with mud and wriggling creatures, and presently he found himself toppled into a wicker cage. He knew he was being carried somewhere.

Soon he made out that he was in a stone house. After

a while, a door opened and he saw standing in a bright light a young girl, graceful, light, and slender, who stretched out her hand to him and led him out of the dark into a great hall with a vast fireplace. When he told the girl his story, tears came to her blue eyes and she showed him a little room where he might hide.

"The witch brought me to this place, too," she said. "I have been her slave. She killed the one who was her slave before me, but before that slave died, she told me about the green stone that the witch has and about how she uses her magic powders.

"Now the witch will kill me and have you for her servant until she tires of you. Then she will catch another. So it has been for many, many years."

Stout Heart was about to tell the girl to run away with him from that dreadful place when they heard the voice of the old witch.

"Hide here," said the girl. "I will get the green stone so that we can fly. With you I dare to do it."

She thrust him into the little room and closed the door. Through the wall he heard the old witch throwing a pile of wood on the hearth.

"I have a new prize," she said. "I have fattened you long enough, girl, and now you must be my meal. One slave at a time is enough for me, and the lad will do. Fetch pepper and salt, lazy one. Lose no time, for I am hungry."

The girl went into another room while the witch fell on her knees and began to build a roaring fire. Soon the girl returned, and as she passed the old woman, she threw something on her. But it was not salt and pepper. It was some of the magic powder.

The hag had no idea what the girl had thrown on her and began to scold her for spilling the salt and pepper. Then, getting to her feet, she threw the girl into the same room where the boy was hiding, not knowing that he was there. She locked the door.

"Wait until I am ready to roast you!" she screamed.

The girl thrust the green stone into the hands of Stout Heart, and at once they flew through the window and out into the open air. As for the old witch, the powder did its work and she began to swell so that she could not get out through any of the doors. But the boy and girl, looking down from high above the house, saw the witch struggling to get out through the thatched roof.

The two lost no time. They flew swift and high. But swift, too, was the old witch. She burst out through the roof, leapt to the ground, and began to run after them. The old witch knew that they must have the green stone, but she was gleeful in her wicked old heart as she watched the sun going down, since the stone would only allow them to fly until sunset.

So she kept on with giant strides and leaps, going so fast that she was always very near the two in the air. Now, as the sun dropped low in the western sky, the girl thought of a plan and, scattering some of the magic powder on the earth, she rejoiced to see that the leaves on which it fell turned into rabbits. The old witch could not resist them and stopped a moment to eat some of the rabbits.

But the hungry old witch soon went on and regained the time she had lost. In a moment she was under them again, running as fast as ever. The girl scattered more powder, this time on some thornbushes, and they changed into foxes. Again the old woman stopped to eat, and the two gained a little. But the sun was sinking lower, and they were dropping nearer to the earth, only a little higher than the treetops. The old woman, leaping after them, could almost touch them.

Ahead of them was the lake in which Stout Heart had been caught, the waters as red as blood in the sunset. The power of the stone was failing, and they had but a small amount of powder left. The old witch was so near that they could hear her breathing and almost felt her terrible claws in their clothing.

The girl threw the last handful of magic powder onto the bank of the lake, and they saw the grass turn to ants and the stones to turtles as they passed over the water so low that their feet touched the surface. The power of the stone was almost gone.

The old witch, seeing the turtles, stopped to swallow them, shells, heads, and all, and that gave the boy and the girl time to reach the opposite shore just as the sun touched the rim of the earth.

The old witch plunged into the lake, for she could travel on water as fast as she could on land. She cut through the water so swiftly that a great wave leapt up on each side of her, and it was clear that before the sun was gone, she would have her claws in the two friends.

But in the middle of the lake, the weight of the turtles she had swallowed began to bear her down. In vain she struggled, making a great uproar and lashing about so furiously that the water became hot and a cloud of steam rose up. The turtles were like great stones inside her, and she sank beneath the water and was seen no more.

Great was the joy of the people when Stout Heart brought the girl to his home. She became his wife and was loved by all in the village as the fairest woman among them.

The Coffin Lid

In Russian folktales there are clear and simple rules for bringing the dead back to life
as well as for keeping a corpse in its grave.

⋙

A peasant was driving along one night with a load
of pots in his cart. His horse grew tired and came to a
standstill at the edge of a graveyard. The peasant un-
harnessed his horse and set it free to graze, while he
himself lay down on one of the graves. For some reason
he couldn't get to sleep.

He lay there wide awake for some time, and suddenly
the grave began to open beneath him. He felt the move-
ment and sprang to his feet. Out of the grave came a
corpse, wrapped in a white shroud and holding a coffin
lid. Yes, the corpse came out, ran to the church, and
laid the coffin lid at the door. Then it set off for the
village.

The peasant was a daring fellow who didn't know
the meaning of fear. He picked up the coffin lid and
went to stand by his cart, waiting to see what would
happen. Before long, the dead man came back and
looked around for his coffin lid, but it was not to be
seen. The corpse searched here and there until he came
up to the peasant.

"Give me my lid," he howled. "If you don't, I'll tear you to bits!"

"What about my hatchet?" answered the peasant. "I'll be chopping you into small pieces!"

"Be a good fellow! Give me back my lid!" begs the corpse.

But the peasant said, "I won't give it back until you tell me where you've been and what you've done."

"Well, I've been in the village and I killed a couple of boys," said the corpse.

"Then tell me how they can be brought back to life," said the peasant.

"I hate to tell you," said the corpse, "but this is what you can do, if you insist. Cut off the left side of my shroud — the *left* side, mind you. When you come into the house where I killed the boys, pour some live coals from the hearth fire into a pot and put the piece of the shroud in with them. Then lock the door. The boys will be revived by the smoke immediately. Now will you give me my lid?"

The peasant cut off the left side of the corpse's shroud and gave him the coffin lid. The corpse went over to his grave, and the grave opened. But just as the dead man was climbing down into it, the cocks began to crow. The corpse didn't have time to get properly covered. One end of the coffin lid was left sticking out of the ground.

The peasant saw all this and took notice of it. Then, as the day began to dawn, he harnessed his horse and

drove into the village. In one of the houses he heard cries and wailing. In he went. There lay two dead boys with their whole family mourning around them.

"Don't cry," says he. "I can bring them to life."

"Do it, friend," said the relatives. "We'll give you half of all we have if you succeed."

The peasant did everything as the corpse had told him, and the boys came back to life. Their relatives were delighted, but just the same, they seized the peasant and tied him up with cords, saying, "No, no, you trickster! We'll hand you over to the law. Since you knew how to bring the boys back to life, maybe it was you who killed them!"

"For the love of God, don't think such a thing, good people!" cried the peasant.

Then he told them everything that had happened to him during the night. Well, they spread the news through the village. Everyone assembled and swarmed into the graveyard. They found the grave from which the dead man had come. They tore it open with their bare hands and pinned down the corpse with an aspen stake right through its heart so that it could never again rise up and kill anyone. Then they rewarded the peasant richly and sent him home with great honor.

The Stone Boat

All over the world we hear of soul-boats that
carry the dead to the next world. In this tale,
a young Canadian Iroquois brave fasts and
keeps ceaseless vigil to find the gateway to
the land of souls and a shining island where
he hopes to be reunited with his lost bride.

ℰℛ

*A*t night, around Iroquois lodge fires, the old men
tell that many years ago, before white men came, there
lived a young hunter, Abeka, who was straight and tall
and keen of eye. He knew all the signs of the forest
and all the woodland paths from the north to the great
falls of Niagara. Some said he could talk to the birds
and the little animals of the woods. He knew the ancient songs of his people, and every young girl in his
village hoped that he would sing love songs to her.

At last he fell in love with a slim, black-haired girl
of his tribe, and their marriage was arranged. The young
hunter brought gifts to the hut of his sweetheart: soft
pelts of deer and beaver, baskets and blankets, beads
and embroideries. All the people of the neighboring
villages were summoned to the wedding feast. But
while the runners were going through the forest, in-
viting the guests, the girl fell ill with a strange sickness.

Even as priests and doctors beat their drums and chanted their magic spells to cure her, the promised bride faded away and died. She was buried by the wailing women in a grove beyond the village.

Winter came. Day after day, Abeka went out with his dog to wander sorrowfully through the frozen forest or to kneel at the grave of his beloved. The old men of his tribe reminded him that he was a famous hunter. They tried to rouse his pride and to cheer him up. But nothing could break through the gloom of his despair. At last the old men called Abeka to the council circle. "There is one way by which you might join your bride," they said. "But no one has ever found the way and returned alive. Are you brave enough to risk your life?"

"I will risk it," answered Abeka.

Then the old men told him what he must do. "Somewhere in the forest is a path that leads from the land of the living to the land of the dead. To see it, you must neither eat nor sleep. Do this, and you may see the path."

Many days and nights Abeka fasted and prayed without rest. One winter night as he sat by the grave of his bride, a dark cloud shut out the moonlight, and in that moment the trees around him disappeared into thin air. Then the shadow was swept away, and there, glittering in a carpet of snow, lay a broad path leading away to the south.

Taking up his bundle of food and his bow and arrows, Abeka set out eagerly, followed by his faithful dog, along this trail of light. Many a day he tramped through the snow and across frozen streams until at last spring came and melted the snow and ice. Now Abeka followed the path under sunny skies, over green hills and through peaceful valleys. New leaves covered the trees, and every branch was alive with bird song. Squirrels chattered at him, and the red fox crossed his path.

Striding happily through this pleasant land, Abeka saw in the distance a great grove of beeches and cedars on a hillside carpeted with flowers. There the path led straight to a lodge. Abeka saw someone standing in the doorway. He ran forward, sure that he had found his bride. But it was not she. It was an old man with snow-white hair. His deep-set eyes were as brilliant as the winter stars. Over his shoulders he wore a robe of skins, and he held a staff in his hand.

Abeka was sick at heart with disappointment. He began to tell of his long journey, but the old man stopped him. "I expected you," he said. "I have come to welcome you. The girl you seek passed this way not long ago and rested here. You, too, must rest, and then I will answer your questions and tell you how to go on."

The young hunter had never felt so hungry and tired. He went into the lodge to eat and soon fell into a deep sleep. When he awoke, he found the old man standing in the doorway.

He spoke to Abeka. "My lodge is the gateway to the land of the dead." He pointed toward the south. "To go there you must cross this plain. The girl you love is now a spirit. To join her, you, too, must become a spirit. You cannot take your body with you. Leave it here with your bow and arrows, your bundle, and your dog. You will find them safe on your return, and all will be well with you."

He laid his withered hand on Abeka's shoulder, and the young man felt a new strength and lightness. He walked toward the plain, and as he went, the birds sang to him. The animals spoke to him in friendship, and the trees raised their branches to let him pass on his way.

All day he traveled joyously until he came to the edge of a broad lake. Far out across its clear waters he saw the shining shores of an island, and he longed to go there. On the near shore lay a strange white canoe, and as he came close, he saw that it was made of stone. For a moment his heart sank, but he remembered the old man's words: *All will be well with you.* Pushing the canoe out into the water, he fearlessly jumped into it.

He had handled birchbark canoes since childhood. Now he balanced himself in his stone boat, seized a strong paddle that lay in it, and drove the blade into the sparkling waters of the lake. The boat seemed to float as if in the sky. Then he saw another canoe approaching. It, too, was of stone, and in it he saw with joy the lost one for whom he had searched so long.

She turned her canoe and, side by side, they paddled toward the island in the lake. Then, as they came

nearer, mountainous waves rushed toward them, and Abeka cried out in fear lest he and his bride should drown. Each wave carried them onward, but behind it there was always another even more terrifying. In the midst of these waves, Abeka saw other canoes overturning. He saw men and women struggling and sinking into the clear depths. Far below were heaps of bones, perhaps the bones of those who had tried and failed to reach the island. Only the canoes of little children met no waves in their journey.

At last Abeka and his bride reached the white beach of the beautiful island. They left their canoes and, hand in hand, wandered happily along its shores. Cold never came to this island. There was no want or sorrow or sickness or starvation. It was always a land of joy. Abeka put his arms around the girl for whom he had longed and traveled so far.

Then he heard a voice like that of a great and good chieftain. "Go back to your own land. Your time has not yet come." And suddenly he remembered the old man in the lodge where he had left his body. He knew that he must return for it, and with this knowledge, his joy turned to bitterness. He fell to his knees on the white sand and buried his face in his hands.

The voice spoke again. "You have duties to your people and deeds left unfinished. You will be the worthy ruler of your tribe for many years. My messenger who keeps the gate will give you back your body and tell you what you must do. Listen to him. You must leave behind you the spirit you have followed. When your work is done, you will come again, for she belongs here now and will forever be as young and as happy as she was when I called her from the land of snows."

Abeka found himself once again in the grove at the edge of his village. All was as it had been. His bow and arrows and his bundle lay on the ground beside him. But on the grave the snow had disappeared. The birds sang to Abeka and the animals spoke to him in friendship as he walked into his village with his faithful dog beside him. His heart was at peace.

Tiny Man

In the bogs of England's East Anglia, before
the fens were drained, there was fear of evil
spirits and the voices of the dead crying in
the mists. But one little spirit had protected
the people, and what would they do if Tiny
Man were driven away by the Dutchies?
Spirits have ways to get even.

~

Aye, the old days are gone by, and folk now know
nothing about Tiny Man. But it's true for all that. I've
seen him myself, limping by in the fog, all gray and
white and screeching like a peewit, but it's a long time
since he's been by. I guess Tiny Man's been frightened
away by the new ways, for I never hear anyone say, as
they did when I was young and anyone had a lot of
trouble, "Ah, you haven't been out at the new moon
lately, and for certain sure, Tiny Man was looking for
you. It's bad luck to cross him . . . Tiny Man without
a name!"

You see, on the east coast of England where the land
is flat, there were once bogs and swamps. It was fen
country, where people lived by hunting and fishing.
Spirits lived there, too, goblins and will-o'-the-wisps
and suchlike. At night you could hear the voices of
dead folk, moaning and crying and beckoning in the

dark. Everyone shook and shivered, partly from ague
and fever, and partly because they saw hands without
arms, and ghostly foxes dancing on the tufts of grass,
and witches riding on the great black snags that raised
their branches out of the dark bog water, twisting like
snakes.

The fen people were terrified of all these things, but
there was one spirit they loved as well as feared: Tiny
Man. And when there was talk of draining the fens,
they were afraid that when the bogs went, Tiny Man
would go, too.

Tiny Man lived in the water holes and only came out
in the evening, when the mists rose. Then he crept out
in the darkling, *limpety lobelty,* with long white hair and
a long white beard all tangled together. He wore a gray
coat, and he came with a sound of running water and
the shrill call of a bird, a peewit, whose call sounds like
a laugh. It was creepy to hear Tiny Man out in the dark,
in the wind and water.

When the season was wet and the water rose to their
very doorsteps, the fen people would go out at the time
of the new moon and call, "Tiny Man without a name,
the water's high!" Then they would wait until they
heard a peewit and would shut the door, knowing that
the high water would go down.

Finally, Dutch workmen were brought in from Hol-
land because they knew all about draining bogs and
building dikes and digging ditches. The Dutchies were
brought in by those who decide such things. The fen

people could not stop the draining. They saw dikes being built and the river bed being changed and the bog lands drying. They were told that ague and fever would go away and there would be good farmland in place of the fens. But they were uneasy, for they were used to the bogs as their fathers had been before them, and they thought, *Bad's bad, but meddling's worse.* They were angry with the Dutch who had come to do the digging. They would not give them food or bedding or kind words, for they said the draining would bring unlucky days to the fens and Tiny Man would not like it.

Mind you, he was not wicked and wild like the Water Wives, or white and creepy like the Dead Hands, and he was real good at times. If the water rose and crept up to the doorsills, fathers and mothers and all the brats would go out in the darkling when the new moon came and call out together, a little scared, just like I told you, "Tiny Man without a name, the water's high!" And they would stand shaking and shivering till they heard the peewit screech across the swamp, and in the morning, sure enough, the water would be down. Tiny Man had done the job.

So as I was saying, Tiny Man lived in the water holes, and the Dutchies were emptying them out. The water holes were almost dry with the water being drawn off into the big ditches and dikes, and the soppy, quivering bog was turning into firm ground, and where would Tiny Man be then? Everybody said that bad times were coming.

But there was no help for it. The Dutchies dug, and the dikes got longer and longer and deeper and deeper, and the water ran away, and the black, soft bog lands would soon be turned into green fields.

Then there was trouble, and in the barnyards and kitchens at home, the folk whispered strange tales. "For sure, trouble comes from crossing Tiny Man." First one and then another of the Dutchies was gone, clean spirited away. Not a shadow of them was ever seen again. Tiny Man had taken them away and drowned them in the mud holes where they hadn't drained out all the water.

And the folk nodded and said, "Aye, that comes of crossing Tiny Man."

More Dutchies were brought in for the work, and though Tiny Man carried them away, the work went on nonetheless, and nothing could stop it. And soon the poor bog folk knew that Tiny Man was angry with them, too. The cows sickened, the pigs starved, the ponies went lame. The new milk turned sour, the thatched roofs fell in, and all went topsy-turvy.

Babies sickened in their mothers' arms. It was like a frost that comes and kills the prettiest flowers. Mothers' hearts were sore with all this sickness and whatnot, and something had to be done.

At last, some of them remembered how when the waters had risen in the marshes before the digging and the folk had called out to Tiny Man when the new moon came, he had heard them and had done what they asked. And they thought maybe if they called him again, to show him that the bog folk wished him well and that they would give him back the water if they only could, maybe he'd take off the bad spell and forgive them again.

So when the new moon came, they all gathered, together with womenfolk and babies, where a ditch met the river. They came by threes and fours, jumping at every sigh of the wind and crying out at every black, twisted snag. But they didn't need to, because the poor old goblins and will-o'-the-wisps had been clean dug away.

However, as I was saying, the people came, every one with a pail of water, and while it grew dark they stood close to each other, whispering and trembling in the shadows and listening to the moaning of the wind and the *lip-lap* of the running water. And when it was full dark, they called out, "Tiny Man without a name, here's water for you. Take your spell away!" And they poured the water out of their pails into the ditch, *splash sploppert!* Then everything was still.

It was scary in that stillness. They listened with all their might to hear if Tiny Man answered them, and there was nothing but unnatural stillness. Then, just when they thought it was no use, there broke out the awfulest wailing and whimpering all around them, like a lot of little crying babies with no one to comfort them. The mothers cried out as if it were their babies calling on Tiny Man to take the spell away and let children live and grow strong. And the poor innocents, floating above in the dark, whimpered softlike as if they knew their mothers' voices and were trying to reach them. And some women said that tiny hands had touched them and cold lips kissed them and soft wings fluttered around them that night as they stood waiting and listening.

Then all at once, there was stillness again and they could hear the water lapping at their feet and the dogs yelping in the barnyards. And then came, soft and fondlike from the river itself, the old peewit call. Once again it came, and sure enough, it was Tiny Man. And they knew the spell was broken, for it was so kind and sorrylike.

How they laughed and cried together, running and jumping about like brats coming out of school, as they set off for home with light hearts. But the mothers thought of their dead babies, and their arms felt empty and their hearts lonesome for the cold kisses and the fluttering of the tiny fingers and the poor little ghosts drifting about in the sighing of the night wind.

But from that day — mark my words! — the sick children got well, and the cattle throve, and the pigs fattened. The men had good wages, and bread was plentiful, for Tiny Man had broken the bad spell. So, every new moon, out they went in the darkling to the nearest ditch — fathers and mothers and brats — and they poured water into the ditch, saying, "Tiny Man without a name, here's water for you!"

And the peewit cry would come back, soft and tender

and pleased. But for certain sure, if one of them didn't go out — unless he was sick — Tiny Man missed him and was angry with him and laid the spell on him harder than ever until he went with the others at the next new moon to ask Tiny Man to break the spell. And when the children were bad, they told them that Tiny Man would get them, and they would be as good as gold, for they knew he would do it.

Those days are gone by, and folk now know nothing about Tiny Man. But it's true for all that. I've seen him myself, limping by in the fog, *limpety lobelty,* all gray and white and screeching like a peewit. But it's a long time since he's been by.

The Bells of Ys

Pronounce it *EES,* but don't look for it if you ever go to France. You *will* see a treacherous bay on the coast of Brittany and jagged rocks three hundred feet high where gigantic waves ceaselessly fling themselves. Sometimes you will hear a mysterious sound of bells, where there are no bells.

༄

At the westernmost tip of Brittany, where French land narrows to a point, a great cliff faces the fury of the Atlantic Ocean. In time of storm, monstrous waves, fifty, sixty, even eighty feet high, tear hungrily at the rocks, as if to devour them, and the Breton sailor prays, "Help me, O Lord! My boat is so small and the sea is so big."

But once, long ago, on that shore there stood a fair and beautiful city called Ys. It was built of stone to last forever, and it was a city of bells. From the stone towers of Ys the bells rang sweetly and softly, marking the hours, calling the people to worship, and warning them in time of danger. In those times there was always danger, and Ys was ringed with a stone wall to protect the city from its enemies by land or by sea.

The sea itself was an enemy, for the tides were very fierce and strong on this coast. Without the protection of the wall, the city would have been overwhelmed by the waves. Two gates pierced the wall, one facing the land and one facing the sea, but only when the tide fell and the sea drew back could the gate toward the sea be opened.

Gralon, the king of Ys, was a good man. From his high palace he loved to look down on his beautiful city, and he loved even more to look at his beautiful daughter, Dahut. She was a strange child. Her eyes were as blue as the sea — and as cold as the sea. Dahut's hair was pale, like the foam that crested on the waves and spread itself on the yellow sands. As she grew older, her temper became as changeable as the moods of the sea. Dahut could bewitch a man's heart with one toss of her fair hair, one look from her deep eyes.

Some folk said that Dahut *was* a witch, for she often visited a rocky little island that could barely be seen on the far horizon, where no one lived except nine old women. The people of Ys feared them, for they were known to gather herbs, mix them with sea foam, and brew them into a potion of magic power.

Ys had reason to fear and hate Dahut. Every young man who looked at her longed for her, and to love Dahut meant death itself. By night she would send a masked henchman to the home of some luckless young man, bringing an invitation to visit her in her palace. None of her lovers ever returned. One by one, they were strangled and their bodies were flung over a cliff into a deep gully.

Near the city lived a hermit, who came to King Gralon and warned him that the wickedness of Dahut would bring Ys to ruin and destruction. "Remember, O King, how it is written, 'If thy heart offend thee, cut out thy heart and cast it from thee.' "

But the king trusted his heart. He could think no evil against his beautiful daughter. Even when the people showed him the bodies of their dead sons, he would only pray for Dahut. He would not control her.

Indeed the king *could* not control Dahut. As a child, she had found her true love, the sea, the only lover strong enough to please her. Therefore Dahut despised all men. Their weakness, compared with the strength of the sea, amused her. This was the secret of her wickedness.

Now, in spite of King Gralon's love for his daughter, he, too, had a secret which he had never told her. Except for the king, only one young man knew where the key to the gate in the seawall was hidden. Like Dahut, this young man, Gavin, had one love, but where her love was the sea, his was the city of Ys. Because he was a hunchback, he did not hope for the love of any woman. Instead, the lonely Gavin turned his thoughts to the beauty of Ys, the whiteness of her towers, the sweetness of her bells. Faithful to the trust the king had given him, Gavin kept the key to the seawall next to his heart.

One spring night, a night of high tide, Dahut walked through the streets of Ys. Above her the bells chimed the hour of midnight and the moonlight shone silver on the sleeping city. But the peaceful scene meant nothing to Dahut. Ys was only a city of men, all weak and worthless. The sea was calling to her.

Swift as the wind, she passed through the narrow streets of the city and climbed to the top of the seawall. There stood the bent figure of a young man. It was Gavin, who often came alone at midnight to look down like a guardian on the city he loved.

Dahut came close to him and spoke his name. Gavin bowed with respect and waited for her orders. To Dahut this was only another weak young man, another victim. "Look at me," she commanded.

Then Gavin saw Dahut's eyes, glittering like cold flames as the waves glittered under the moonlight. She turned and looked down at the city, and Gavin was afraid, not for himself but for Ys. Without thinking, he put his hands to his heart, and at once, by the power of witch's magic, Dahut knew that the key to the seawall was hidden there.

She put her arms around Gavin, but there was no warmth in her embrace, and he tried to free himself. "Give me the key," she whispered.

Then Gavin felt Dahut's cold fingers at his throat, tighter and tighter, strangling him. The key was in her hand, and with failing strength he tried to wrest it from her. Then a mist covered his eyes. For the last time Gavin heard the bells of Ys ringing as Dahut threw his body into the sea.

Down the steps she ran from the top of the seawall to its gate. She thrust the key into the lock, turned it, and pushed with all her force against the heavy gate. Slowly it opened. The tide was rising; already the black water covered the sands. The water surged, roaring through the open gate and into the city streets. Dahut ran back toward her father's palace, and behind her raced the sea.

The people of Ys began to waken at the sound of the waters. The bell ringer pealed a warning, but it was too late. Only on the higher ground where the king's palace stood was there any hope of escape. From a tower window King Gralon looked out and saw the wild sea raging over the city. He ran to his stable, mounted his swift horse Morwark, and set spurs to its sides. Then above the thunder of the water he heard Dahut's laugh and her shrill voice: "Father! Take me with you!" He knew at once that she had opened the sea gate.

King Gralon remembered the words of the hermit: *If thy heart offend thee, cut out thy heart and cast it from thee.* But he stretched out his hand and pulled his daughter up behind him. He felt her cold arms clinging to him as his horse galloped through the landward gate. And still the sea followed, rising higher and higher.

As he rode, King Gralon looked back over his shoulder. The sea had covered the city. Ys was gone. "My people, I have betrayed you!" cried the king.

When they reached the great cliff that towered over Ys, Dahut's white hand pointed downward. In the black, tormented sea tossing below, the king saw the ghostly faces of the young men who had died for the love of his beautiful daughter. Then he heard behind him the laughter of Dahut.

At that sound, the horse Morwark neighed and reared. With one mighty effort the king freed himself from his daughter's grasp. She fell from the horse, plunged over the edge of the cliff, and vanished into the sea. At once, the waves grew quiet, as if they had found what they sought.

Sick at heart, King Gralon rode away from the lost city of Ys and made a new capital at Quimper, a city which stands to this day. There, between the towers of the cathedral, is a statue of the king riding his great horse Morwark. The king's ghost still wanders through the villages of Brittany, putting kind and gentle thoughts into the hearts of Breton girls.

As for the Breton fisherman, mending his nets by the fire, on gusty nights when the wind moans, he may hear a knock at the door. When he opens it and finds no one there, he says, "That was not the wind. That was one of Dahut's lovers looking for his home."

And in fine weather, when the sun sparkles on the sea, a sailor, looking down from his little boat into the depths of the bay where Ys once stood, may hear the sound of bells or see below him the stone towers of the drowned city of Ys. And if the man is without sin, they say that Ys will rise from the sea before his eyes, with all its sweet bells ringing.

The Haunted Harp

From the lowlands of Scotland comes this tale with its eerie thread of music — not sweet, but menacing. Murder will out!

༄

*O*nce there were two king's daughters who lived near the bonny milldams of Binnorie. And a young knight named Sir William came wooing the elder princess and won her love. As tokens of true love he gave her a pair of gloves and a ring. But after a time he began to look at the younger sister with her cherry red cheeks and golden hair, and his love went out to her so that he cared no longer for the other one. The elder princess hated her sister for taking away Sir William's love, and day by day her hate grew and grew and she plotted and she planned how to get rid of her. So one fine morning, fair and clear, she said to her sister, "Let us go and see our father's boats come in at the bonny millstream of Binnorie."

The sisters went there hand in hand. And when they came to the river's bank, the younger one got up on a stone to watch for the boats. And her sister, coming behind her, caught her around the waist and pushed her into the rushing millstream of Binnorie.

"O sister, sister, reach me your hand!" the younger

princess cried as she floated away. "Save me, and you shall have half of all I've got or shall get!"

"No, sister, I'll reach you no hand of mine, for I am the heir to all your land. I will never touch the hand that has come between me and my own heart's love."

"O sister, O sister, then reach me your glove!" wailed the younger sister as she floated farther away. "I promise you shall have your William again."

"No hand or glove of mine you'll touch," cried the cruel princess. "Sweet William will be all mine when you are sunk beneath the bonny millstream of Binnorie." And she turned and went home to the king's castle.

And the younger princess floated down the millstream, sometimes swimming and sometimes sinking, till she came near the mill. Now the miller's daughter was cooking that day and needed water for her cooking. And as she went to draw it from the stream, she saw something floating toward the milldams, and she called out, "Father! Father! Close the dams! There's something white — a mermaid or a milk white swan — coming down the stream."

So the miller hastened to the dams and stopped the heavy, cruel mill wheels. Then they took the princess from the water and laid her on the bank of the river.

Fair and beautiful she looked as she lay there. In her golden hair were pearls and precious stones. Around her waist was her golden girdle, and the golden fringe

of her white dress came down over her lily feet. But she was drowned, drowned!

And as she lay there in her beauty, a famous harper passed by the milldam of Binnorie and saw her sweet pale face. Though he traveled on far away, he could not forget that face, and after many days he came back to the bonny millstream of Binnorie. But all he could find of the princess where they had put her to rest were her bones and her golden hair.

So he made a harp out of her breastbone and her hair, and he traveled on up the hill from the milldam of Binnorie till he came to the castle of the king, her father.

That night they were all gathered in the castle hall to hear the great harper — the king and queen, their daughter and son, and Sir William and all their court. And first the harper sang with his old harp, making them joyful and glad, or making them sorrow and weep, just as he chose.

But while he sang, he put the harp he had made that day on a stone in the hall. And presently it began to sing by itself, low and clear, and the harper stopped and all were hushed.

And this is what the harp sang:

> *Oh, yonder sits my father, the king,*
> *Binnorie, O Binnorie;*
> *And yonder sits my mother, the queen,*
> *By the bonny milldams o' Binnorie.*

And yonder stands my brother, Hugh,
Binnorie, O Binnorie;
And by him my William, false and true,
By the bonny milldams o' Binnorie.

Then they all wondered, and the harper told them how he had seen the princess lying drowned on the riverbank near the bonny milldams of Binnorie, and how he had afterward made this harp out of her hair and breastbone. Just then the harp began singing again, and this is what it sang out loud and clear:

And there sits my sister who drowned me
By the bonny milldams o' Binnorie.

And the harp snapped and broke and never sang more.

The Golem

Prague was once the capital of Bohemia, now part of Czechoslovakia. Much of the old city remains today, but one part is gone — the ghetto. Only a few buildings, including the old synagogue, still stand there as a reminder of a bleak time in history. Jewish people all over the world still talk about the good Rabbi Loew of Prague, who used occult powers to protect his people and who produced the golem.

☙

Long ago in Prague, the Jews lived along the river Moldau, separated by a high stone wall from the rest of the old Bohemian city. The city's magistrates had always kept the ancient gates in the wall open — until evil times came. When a plague swept through the land or when the crops failed, the Christians looked for someone to blame. Without reason, they would blame the Jews.

Over time, hatred and fear grew together. It was said that the Jews killed Christian children, and the magistrates of Prague ordered the gates in the wall to be closed and locked at night. And it was ordered that during the day, all Jews must wear yellow badges when they left their ghetto.

Now the good Rabbi Judah Loew was a wise man. He not only read the holy books, but he studied the stars and understood the mystery of numbers. And seeing the troubles of the innocent Jews, he prayed to heaven for a way to help his people. The answer came in a dream.

Accordingly, Rabbi Loew sent for two young men, his son-in-law, Isaac, and his favorite pupil, Jacob, and said, "Our people must have a protector. Let us make a golem. We will mold clay into the shape of a man, and we will bring it to life. Fire, water, and air must work on the clay. You, Isaac, were born under the constellation of Fire, and you, Jacob, under the constellation of Water. I myself was born under the constellation of Air. With Fire, Water, and Air we will make our golem live."

The three purified themselves by washing and by prayer. They went by night to the bank of the river Moldau, and there they molded clay into the figure of a man, ten feet long. Rabbi Loew ordered Isaac to walk around the figure seven times, from left to right, saying magic words. As Isaac did so, the figure glowed red as fire.

Then it was Jacob's turn. He walked seven times around the figure, saying different magic words, and water quenched the fire. Hair grew on the golem's head, and nails grew on its fingers and toes. Then Rabbi Loew walked once around the figure and put into its mouth a strip of parchment on which was written the name of God.

Finally all three men recited the words from the Bible that describe how the first human being was made of clay and brought to life by God: "And He breathed into his nostrils the breath of life, and man became a living soul." At these words the golem opened his eyes, and Rabbi Loew ordered him to stand up. The rabbi gave him clothes and took him home to his own house.

The golem could not speak, but he did what he was told to do, and on the Sabbath, he went to the synagogue, where he seemed to enjoy the singing. The rabbi named him Joseph.

At first, the rabbi's wife sent Joseph on errands, until one day in the marketplace, the fruit woman laughed at the strange fellow. The golem picked her up, apples, fruit stall and all, and ran through the ghetto, while everyone laughed. Another time, when the rabbi's wife sent the golem to the well for a pail of water, he could not be stopped but ran to and fro with water until the house was flooded.

After that, Joseph's usual task was to light household fires for the Sabbath, and this he did for all the families in the ghetto. But his real work was to protect the people. The rabbi gave the golem a charm on a chain. When Joseph wore the charm around his neck, he became invisible. He could then be sent out through the streets of the ghetto to watch for trouble. Sometimes at night, he would see a Christian inside the gates laying a dead child at the doorway of a house. Then the golem would run to Rabbi Loew and lead him to the spot, telling by gestures what he had seen. If the Jewish householder was accused of killing the child, the rabbi would appear in court with the facts discovered by the golem. Rabbi Loew was so much respected that when he gave evidence, an innocent man would be set free.

Finally, King Rudolph, who ruled over Bohemia, heard of the rabbi's good work and made it illegal for a Jew to be accused of killing Christian children. The king knew that such charges were nonsense.

One Friday, Rabbi Loew decided that the golem was no longer needed and began to think of turning him back into a lump of clay. But while he was considering this, he forgot to give the golem his orders for the next day. Without his usual orders, the golem did not know what to do.

Suddenly, he jumped up and lit all the fires in the rabbi's house. Then he ran out into the streets of the ghetto, lighting fires everywhere. The people ran after him, screaming, "Stop him! Stop the golem! He has gone mad!" But no one could catch him. The golem pulled up trees for firewood. He not only lit fires on hearths; he set fire to houses.

Rabbi Loew was praying in the synagogue when he heard the commotion outside. He ran out and saw the golem rushing down the street with burning branches in each hand.

"Stop, Joseph! Stop! Come here at once!" cried the rabbi. And the golem stopped. He came back and stood quietly before the rabbi. "Go home, Joseph," said Rabbi Loew. "Go home and go to bed." The golem obeyed.

That night Rabbi Loew called his son-in-law, Isaac, and his favorite pupil, Jacob, to his house. He told them what they must do.

The three men went to the room where the golem was sleeping. Isaac walked seven times around the bed, speaking the same words he had said on the night when the golem was made. This time, he said the words backward, and he walked from right to left. Then it was Jacob's turn. He, too, walked from right to left and repeated his magic words backward. Last of all, Rabbi Loew walked around the golem, and all three men recited, backward, the words of creation from the Bible. The rabbi took the piece of parchment out of the golem's mouth, and in an instant there was nothing but a lump of clay lying on the bed. They wrapped it in old prayer robes and carried it to the attic of the synagogue, where they hid it under piles of leaves from old Hebrew books.

The next day, Rabbi Loew sent word to all the people of the ghetto that they were forbidden to go into the attic of the synagogue because of the danger of fire. Everyone knew that there were many old papers there, so the order seemed only reasonable. No one ever went into the attic of the synagogue, and no one ever saw the golem again, alive or dead.

Lord of the Dead

Perfect love and complete devotion are the womanly qualities extolled in this famous story from the *Mahabharata*, the great Sanskrit epic of India, written two thousand years ago. Behind the story lies the ancient Hindu practice in which a widow sacrificed herself on her husband's funeral pyre.

✎

There was once an Indian rajah who ruled over his lands wisely and well. He gave freely to the poor, and his people loved him. He had a beautiful wife. His palaces were filled with treasures: gold, silks, ivory, and jewels. He owned many horses and camels and elephants. Yet he was not happy, because he had no children.

Year after year he offered sacrifices to divine Savitri, praying that he might be blessed with children, and at long last the goddess appeared to him in flames. "Your wish is granted, O virtuous prince," she said. "Your wife will bear a child."

And so it came to pass. The rajah's wife gave birth to a daughter who grew to be the loveliest of princesses. She was named Savitri in honor of the goddess, and indeed she was so like a goddess in beauty of mind and body that no man dared to ask for her hand in marriage.

At last her father said, "Choose for yourself the man you can love, my child. Find a husband worthy of your royal blood, whoever he may be, and I will bless your marriage."

So Savitri set out in a royal procession through the wide lands of India. She traveled to great cities and visited the courts of many rajahs, whose sons would have given all they had to be her husband, but she found no man who could move her heart — until she came to a deep forest where a blind hermit lived with his wife and son. There she stopped to rest and to hear their story.

The hermit had been a rajah himself until he became blind and was driven from his country by an enemy. He and his faithful wife had fled to the forest with their infant son, Satyavan, who had now grown to manhood. Satyavan was as fearless and strong as the wild animals he loved, and he was devoted to his elderly parents. Savitri saw that he cared for them tenderly. She saw that he was as handsome as a god. And to Satyavan the princess looked like a dream from paradise. Her voice echoed in his heart long after she had gone.

Savitri lost no time in returning to her father's palace. With the rajah was his adviser, who was a wise man and a prophet.

"Father," said Savitri, "I have found the man whom I choose for my husband. He is Satyavan, the son of a rajah whose lands have been stolen from him by a usurper. Prince Satyavan lives in a forest hermitage with his father and mother. He brings them fruit and game from the forest, keeps their sacrificial fire burning, and makes their bed soft with fragrant grasses. Such love and tenderness can only come from a gentle heart. This is the man who has won my love."

But the prophet shook his head. "Do not choose Satyavan, princess. True, he is brave and noble, the finest young prince in all India, but a fearful fate hangs over his head. The gods have doomed him to die within one year."

Savitri grew pale, but then she answered, "Whether Satyavan lives long or dies today, my heart has chosen him. It cannot change, and you, father, have given your promise to let me choose my husband."

The rajah frowned. "Child," he said, "I beg you to choose again. Remember that a widow must end her own life when her husband dies. Think, the noblest princes in India would be honored by marriage to you. Choose a long life in a palace, not a short year in a forest hermitage."

But Savitri answered only, "I have chosen, and I know my father will not break his promise."

With a heavy heart, her father gave his consent to Savitri's choice. She was dressed in her bridal robes of silk embroidered with gold. She wore a necklace of priceless pearls. Her rings and bracelets were heavy with jewels. Seated under a canopy on the back of an elephant and followed by a long procession of courtiers and servants, she set off with her father and mother to the forest where Satyavan lived.

Near the hermitage, the rajah ordered a halt and

went forward alone on foot. Satyavan had gone to cut firewood in the forest, but his father and mother offered the rajah their simple hospitality. They were amazed when he said, "I have come to ask that you give your approval to my daughter's marriage with your son. She has told me that he is strong and brave, truthful, generous, and tenderhearted, and she has given him her undying love."

Satyavan's father answered, "In better days I could have wished that my son might marry your daughter, but now he should not take her from a royal palace to live in a forest hut."

The rajah replied, "Your son is Savitri's choice. Her happiness depends on being his wife. Can you and I deny her that happiness?"

"Then may the gods bless her," said Satyavan's father. "My son will hardly believe what has happened, for he has loved your daughter from the first moment he saw her, but he thought that his love was hopeless."

When Satyavan came from his work in the forest, he was bewildered by the news that his father gave him and by the appearance of Savitri leading her royal procession. No shadow dimmed his joy nor the celebration of their wedding day in the forest, for Savitri kept hidden what she knew. Her father and mother said their farewells. Then she took off her royal robes and gladly put on the rough dress that suited her new life in the forest as the devoted wife of Satyavan. She treated his parents with the loving respect of a daughter.

The gods seemed to have blessed Satyavan above all men. Savitri, too, would have been blissfully happy if it had not been for the dark secret she kept hidden as days, weeks, and months passed.

All too soon the year drew to its close. Four days before the fateful date when Satyavan was doomed to die, Savitri began to fast and do penance in the hope that the gods might grant her some wisdom or blessing equal to her need. Day and night she sat beneath a tree, neither eating nor drinking, but the gods sent no answer to her prayers. Satyavan and his parents begged her to rest and break her fast, but she spoke no word and did not move.

At dawn of the fourth day, as Satyavan was about to go into the forest, Savitri said to her husband, "I have only one wish. If you will let me go with you today, tonight I will break my fast."

"The paths are too rough for your little feet," he answered. "Besides, you are weak with fasting and there may be dangers in the forest. Stay here with my parents where you are safe."

But Savitri begged so earnestly that at last Satyavan consented to take her with him, and she walked close by his side along the forest paths as he filled a basket with wild fruits, talking to her and smiling as he worked.

Suddenly he dropped the basket and clasped his head in his hands, saying, "What is the matter? A thousand needles are piercing my brain." He fell to the ground and lay pale and still.

Heartsick, Savitri knelt beside him, holding him in her arms, her head bowed over his.

When she looked up, she saw a strange and terrible figure looking down at them. His garments were blood red; his eyes were like burning coals. In his hand he carried a noose.

Gently laying her husband on the ground, Savitri stood before this awful being. "Who are you?" she whispered. "And what do you want?"

"I am Yama, Lord of the Dead," he answered. "I did not send one of my servants to carry away the soul of Satyavan. I myself have come because he was the noblest of all princes. Let him go, princess. He must depart."

In spite of Savitri's tears and prayers, Yama slipped the noose around the neck of Satyavan and drew it tight. As Satyavan's last breath came from his mouth, his soul came out with it — no bigger than a man's thumb — and Yama closed his fist around it. Then he walked away into the shadows. But not alone. Behind him came Savitri, still begging and pleading.

"Go back," said Yama. "No living person goes where I am going. Go back and prepare for your husband's funeral."

"Wherever you take my lord, I shall go, too," said Savitri. "Since I cannot leave him, I must go with you." And on she went, following in Yama's footsteps.

At last the Lord of the Dead pitied her and said, "Return, my child. The kingdom of Yama is no place

for you. But I will give you whatever you wish, except for the life that I am taking away."

"Then let my husband's father have back his sight and his lands," said Savitri.

"It shall be done," said Yama. "I grant it because of your love and faithfulness. Now turn back. Your little feet are weary and you will die on the long road that lies ahead."

"I am not tired," said Savitri. "Wherever Satyavan goes, I must go." Her feet were torn by sharp thorns and bruised by stones, but on she went behind the Lord of the Dead until he turned and said, "You will soon be lost in the dark. Only return home and I will grant you another wish — anything except this life that I hold in my hand."

Savitri thought of her own parents whose only child was now following in the footsteps of Death. "Give my father princely sons to rule after him," she said.

"So be it," said Yama. "Now go back to light and life."

But Savitri answered, "I cannot go, mighty one. In your hand you are carrying not only my husband's life, but my heart. I must come with you."

Then she saw before her the entrance to a cavern. Hungry wolves and jackals howled in the darkness; she heard the beat of wings and the strange cries of owls and bats. Yama's steps were bent toward the cavern. Once more he turned to Savitri, saying, "Go, child. I cannot bear to have you following me into this place, for if you do, you will die. I grant you one more wish, if only you will leave me."

Savitri bowed her head over the dark hand that held the soul of her husband. "Then give me children — the children of Satyavan," she said. "Let me bear children as good and true as their father."

Yama's eyes were filled with pity. "I grant it," he said. "You have tricked me. Since a Hindu woman can have only one husband, take your Satyavan. Long shall he live and rule with you at his side. His children shall bless you as their mother." He put the soul of Satyavan into Savitri's hand and disappeared into the dark cavern.

Savitri ran all the long, dark way back through the forest until she reached Satyavan's body lying cold and lifeless on the ground. Gently she put her hand across his mouth, and his lips moved. His color returned. He opened his eyes.

"I have had a strange dream," said Satyavan. "A frightful dream. How thankful I am to awake and find you at my side."

"Come, beloved," said Savitri. "All sorrow is past. Take my hand and lead me home."

And it all came to pass as the Lord of the Dead had promised. On the death of his father, Satyavan became rajah over broad lands, with Savitri at his side. Even today, every child in India knows the story of Savitri, the peerless wife, whose love was stronger than death.

Snow

A taboo is a forbidding. Some things must not be done. Some words must not be spoken. Forgetfulness or carelessness is no excuse, especially when the taboo comes from the Other World, the spirit world, as this Japanese tale proves.

ೞ

*I*n a Japanese village there lived two woodcutters, an old man and his apprentice, Minokichi, a lad of eighteen years. Every day they went to work in a forest about five miles from their village. On the way to that forest there was a wide river that could only be crossed by ferryboat. Several times a bridge had been built to replace the ferry, but eventually each bridge had been carried away by a flood.

The old man and the boy were on their way home one very cold evening, when a great snowstorm overtook them. They reached the ferry and found that the boatman had gone away, leaving his boat on the other side of the river. It was no time for swimming, so the woodcutters took shelter in the ferryman's hut, thinking themselves lucky to find any shelter at all.

There was no place in which to make a fire. It was only a small hut with a single door and no window. The woodcutters fastened the door and lay down to rest with their straw raincoats over them. At first they did not feel very cold, and they thought that the storm would soon be over.

The old man fell asleep almost immediately, but the boy, Minokichi, lay awake a long time, listening to the awful wind and the continual slashing of the snow against the door. The river was roaring, and the hut swayed like a boat at sea. It was a terrible storm. The air was becoming colder every moment, and Minokichi shivered under his raincoat. But at last, in spite of the cold, he, too, fell asleep.

He was awakened by a shower of snow in his face. The door of the hut had been forced open, and by the snow-light he saw a woman in the room, a woman all in white. She was bending above the old woodcutter, blowing her breath upon him, and her breath was like a bright white smoke. Almost in the same moment she turned to Minokichi and stooped over him.

He tried to cry out but found that he could not utter any sound. The white woman bent down over him, lower and lower, until her face almost touched him, and he saw that she was very beautiful, though her eyes made him afraid.

For a little time she continued to look at him. Then she smiled, and she whispered, "I intended to treat you like the other man. But I cannot help feeling some pity for you, because you are so young. You are a handsome boy, Minokichi, and I will not hurt you now. But, if

you ever tell anybody — even your own mother — about what you have seen this night, I shall know it, and then I will kill you. Remember what I say!"

With these words, she turned from him and passed through the doorway. Then Minokichi found himself able to move, and he sprang up and looked out. But the woman was nowhere to be seen, and the snow was driving furiously into the hut.

Minokichi closed the door and secured it by fixing several chunks of wood against it. He wondered if the wind had blown it open. Then he thought that he might have been only dreaming and might have mistaken the gleam of the snow-light in the doorway for the figure of a white woman, but he could not be sure. He called to the old woodcutter and was frightened because there was no answer. He put out his hand in the dark and touched the old man's face, and found that it was icy. The old woodcutter was stone cold and dead.

By dawn the storm was over. When the ferryman returned to his hut a little after sunrise, he found Minokichi lying senseless beside the frozen body of the old woodcutter. The ferryman revived Minokichi, and took care of him, but Minokichi remained ill a long time from the effects of the cold of that terrible night. He had been greatly frightened also by the old man's death, but he said nothing about the vision of the white woman.

As soon as he got well again, he returned to his work, going alone every morning to the forest and coming back at nightfall with his bundles of wood, which his mother helped him to sell.

One evening in the winter of the following year, as he was on his way home, he overtook a girl who happened to be traveling by the same road. She was a tall, slim girl, very good-looking, and she answered Minokichi's greeting in a voice as pleasant to the ear as the voice of a songbird.

He walked beside her, and they began to talk. The girl told Minokichi that her name was O-Yuki, which meant snow. She said that she had recently lost both of her parents and was going to a city where she had some poor relations, who might help her to find work as a servant.

Minokichi soon felt charmed by this unknown girl, and the more he looked at her, the more handsome she appeared to be. He asked her whether she was engaged to be married, and she answered laughingly that she was free. Then, in her turn, she asked Minokichi whether he was married or pledged to marry, and he told her that although he had only a widowed mother to support, the question of a daughter-in-law had not yet been considered, as he was very young.

They walked on for a long while without speaking, but as the old saying goes, When the wish is there, the eyes can say as much as the mouth. By the time they reached the village, they had become very much pleased with each other. Minokichi asked O-Yuki to rest a while at his house. After some shy hesitation, she went there with him. His mother made her welcome and prepared a warm meal for her. O-Yuki behaved so nicely that Minokichi's mother took a fancy to her and persuaded her to delay her journey to the city. And the natural end of the matter was that O-Yuki never went to the city at all. She remained in the house as the "honorable daughter-in-law."

O-Yuki proved to be a very good daughter-in-law. When Minokichi's mother died, some five years later, her last words were words of affection and praise for the wife of her son. And O-Yuki bore Minokichi ten children, boys and girls — handsome children, all of them, and very fair of skin.

The country folk thought O-Yuki a wonderful person, by nature different from themselves. Most of the peasant women aged early, but O-Yuki, even after becoming the mother of ten children, looked as young and fresh as on the day when she had first come to the village.

One night, after the children had gone to sleep, O-Yuki was sewing by the light of a paper lamp, and Minokichi, watching her, said, "To see you sewing there, with the light on your face, makes me think of a strange thing that happened when I was a lad of eighteen. I saw someone as beautiful and white as you are now. Indeed, she was very like you."

Without lifting her eyes from her work, O-Yuki responded, "Tell me about her. Where did you see her?"

Then Minokichi told her about the terrible night in

the ferryman's hut, and about the white woman that had stooped above him, smiling and whispering, and about the silent death of the old woodcutter. And he said, "Asleep or awake, that was the only time I saw a being as beautiful as you. Of course, she was not a human being, and I was afraid of her — very much afraid — but she was so white! Indeed, I have never been sure whether it was a dream that I saw or a woman of the snow."

O-Yuki flung down her sewing and arose. She bowed above Minokichi where he sat and shrieked into his face, "It was I! I! I! It was O-Yuki! And I told you then that I would kill you if you ever said one word about it! If it were not for those children asleep there, I would kill you this moment! You had better take very, very good care of them, for if ever they have reason to complain of you, I will treat you as you deserve!"

But even as she screamed, her voice became thin, like a crying of wind. Then she melted into a bright white mist that spiraled to the roof beams, and shuddered away through the smoke hole. Never again was she seen.

The Kindly Ghost

The ghost of a hermit from a desert land in
Africa gives a bag of bones and a bit of advice:
"Wish no evil thing, for evil will fall on the
head of him who conceives it."

༄

*T*hree brothers were wandering in a thirsty land, looking for water. It was hot, very hot. All the springs had
dried up, and their thirst grew greater and greater. So
they came to a tree and sat down under it, for though
all its leaves were withered, its branches gave a little
shade.

And under that tree, the youngest brother, whose
name was Jiri, fell asleep.

Then the eldest brother said to the second brother,
"If we get up and go on, maybe we shall find a little
water. But the water may not be enough to quench the
thirst of all three of us. See, there is Jiri — he is half
dead already. What is the use of dragging him with us?
Let us leave him here to die in peace, and let us go on
without him."

So they got up and walked on, leaving Jiri under the
tree.

Then, little by little, the shadows of the tree branches
shifted as the sun moved through the heavens. The

shadows no longer fell on the sleeping Jiri. And the rays of the sun blazed down on him.

When Jiri woke up, thirst was raging in him. He was so weak that he couldn't stand up. "Brothers!" he called. "Brothers!"

But there was no answer. And then Jiri knew that his brothers had left him to die.

So he folded his hands on his breast and closed his eyes.

Plop! Something fell onto Jiri's folded hands. It was a big, juicy fruit that had been hidden among the withered leaves of the tree and had become so ripe and heavy that it had had to fall.

Jiri ate the fruit, and a little strength returned to him. He scrambled painfully up the tree and found two more fruits. And when he had eaten these, he felt as strong as ever he had felt in his life. "Oh, blessed tree! Oh, blessed tree!" he said. And he bowed down to the ground in front of it.

And now — what was this? The trunk of the tree opened, and Jiri went inside and found a little room. And in that room was an ax, and a bow and a sheaf of arrows. With the ax Jiri cut bark from the tree and made rope snares and caught some little animals. With the bow and arrows he shot some game. And when he thirsted he climbed the tree, where another fruit and yet another were waiting for him to gather.

Then the tree let fall its withered leaves, and Jiri gathered them up and carried them into the room in-

side the trunk to make himself a bed. And so he lived —
all alone in that desert place where no rain fell.

One day he caught a rat in his snare. And the rat
said to him, "Brother, what use am I as food? Let me
go, and there may come a time when I can repay you."

"Go," said Jiri. "My blessing go with you."

And he let the rat go.

The next day he found a hawk in his snare. "Brother,"
said the hawk, "my flesh is but carrion. Set me free,
and there may come a day when I can repay you."

"Go," said Jiri. "My blessing go with you!"

And he set the hawk free.

That night, when he went into the room in the tree
to sleep, he saw the ghost of an old gray man standing
by his bed.

"Jiri," said the old gray ghost, "have you all that your
heart can desire?"

"Not all," said Jiri. "But enough."

"Jiri," said the old gray ghost, "in life I was a hermit
and lived in this tree, pondering day and night on mys-
teries and marvels. And at last I gained such skill in
magic that I had but to raise a finger and all that I willed
to happen did happen. But of what use to me is my
earthly magic in the world of worlds, where what is
ours comes to us of its own accord? And so, Jiri, take
this little pouch. In it are the bones of my earthly
fingers. You have but to throw the pouch on the ground
and wish, and what you wish will become yours. But
see that you wish no evil thing, for evil will fall on the

head of him who conceives it. That is the law of laws that a man defies at his peril. Now sleep, my lad. And in the morning, wish your wish."

So before Jiri's eyes the gray ghost faded. He was a vapor; he was the shadow of a shadow; he was gone. And Jiri lay down and slept.

In the morning he took the little pouch full of bones, went to stand under the tree, and threw the pouch on the ground. "I wish for a village," he said. "A village with springs of water and fields of grain, a village where all the people are kind and friendly."

Immediately he heard the pretty tricklings of springs and streams of water, the lowing of cattle, and the chatter of laughing voices. The withered tree disappeared, the desert land disappeared, and where these things had been stood a village of gaily decorated straw huts, surrounded by grain fields and pasture fields. There were people there, some of them cutting the grain, some plowing with yoked oxen, some going in and out of the straw huts. And when they saw Jiri, these people dropped their tools and their plow handles and their baskets and ran to greet him, crying out, "Welcome to your village, Jiri! Welcome! Welcome!"

And they led him to a hut larger and more beautifully decorated than all the rest and set food before him and brought him a pretty, laughing girl to be his wife.

So Jiri lived in his village happily for a long time. And then one night the kindly ghost of the old gray man came to him again and said, "Jiri, are you content?"

"Yes," said Jiri, "I am content." And he bowed to the ground before the kindly ghost and said, "Will you take back your pouch of bones, for I have nothing left to wish for?"

"Nay, keep it," said the kindly ghost. "But guard it well, for I think you may still have need of it."

And one evening, soon after this, as Jiri sat with his pretty, laughing wife at his hut door in the cool of the evening, he looked along the track that led to the village and saw two weary, ragged, dust-begrimed travelers limping toward him. When the travelers drew near, he saw that they were his two brothers.

And his two brothers fell on their knees and kissed Jiri's feet and cried, "We pray you, noble sir, to give us a little bread and a little water, or we die."

But Jiri raised them up and embraced them, and the tears flowed from his eyes in his joy and pity. He fetched his pouch of bones, flung it on the ground, and said, "I wish a beautiful hut here for my brothers. I wish that the grime be washed from their bodies. I wish them clothed in gay garments. I wish meat and drink to be spread before them, and that of the best."

And as Jiri wished these things, so they happened. The brothers, cleansed of their dirt and dust and clothed in gay garments, sat in a beautiful hut and ate and drank. But now, recognizing Jiri, they were very ill at ease.

So the eldest brother said, "Indeed, Jiri, we thought you had died under that tree, and we had no means of burying your body."

And the second brother said, "We were near death ourselves and too weak to carry you with us."

So they tried to excuse themselves, but Jiri laughed and said, "All that is forgotten. Indeed, my brothers, you did me a good turn; for if you had not left me I should never have met with my good fortune."

And in the fullness of his heart he told them all about the kindly ghost and the pouch of bones.

The brothers bit their lips and squinted with jealousy. Should Jiri, the youngest of the three of them, possess such a treasure and they be at his mercy to do good or harm to as he chose? *No, no,* thought the eldest, *it is* I, *by right of birth, who should possess that treasure!* So he said, "In all humbleness, may we see that pouch?"

Then Jiri fetched the pouch and put it in his brother's hand. "If you desire something, you have but to throw this on the ground and wish," said he.

The eldest brother flung the pouch on the ground and shouted, "Let this village and all who are in it, except Jiri, be moved to a far place. And let there be a desert here, and let Jiri be left wandering in it!"

No sooner said than done. The village melted away; the grain fields, the pasture fields melted away; there were no gaily decorated huts; there were no happy people laughing and singing at their work: there was only a barren desert, and in the desert stood Jiri, all alone.

"Oh my benefactor, my benefactor," cried Jiri, stretching out his arms, "tell me what I must do!"

But no voice answered him; no kindly ghost appeared. The kindly ghost possessed no foot of ground on earth, except where his pouch of bones was laid. And Jiri's eldest brother held that pouch of bones tight in his wicked fist.

And far away across the desert, where the village now stood, the eldest brother and the second brother leered at one another.

"Now we shall live like kings," said they. "Everything is ours, and if we need more, we have only to wish for it."

Yes, everything was theirs: theirs was the pretty trickling of springs and streams of water, theirs the lowing cattle, theirs the pasture fields and the grain fields, theirs the gaily decorated huts. But the people who plowed and reaped and moved in and out of those huts were not laughing; they went about with sullen faces. And Jiri's pretty wife sat at her hut door and wept.

The brothers hung the pouch of bones on the roof pole inside their hut, and all night long the kindly ghost moved about the hut sighing and groaning, so that the brothers could not sleep. Finally the eldest brother flew into a rage, flung the bones on the hut floor, and shouted, "I wish you to go, you stupid ghost, and trouble us no more!"

Then the kindly ghost fled away. And the eldest brother hung up the pouch of bones on the roof pole again and laughed.

Now all this time Jiri was wandering in the desert, searching for his village. Sometimes he thought he could see the far-off gleaming of its huts, and sometimes he thought he could hear the trickling of its springs. And toward those sights and sounds he would run. But though he ran all day he could never get nearer to them.

And one day, utterly discouraged, he sat himself down on a hummock of sand and wept. And then at his feet a little voice squeaked, "Jiri! Jiri!" And out of the hummock of sand a little quivering snout appeared and then a little furry body, and a little creature gave a leap and sprang onto Jiri's knee.

It was the rat that Jiri had long ago caught in a snare and set free again with his blessing.

"Jiri, why do you weep?"

"I weep for my pretty, laughing wife and for my village and for my pouch of bones that my brothers have stolen from me."

And he told the rat all about it.

The rat said, "Wait, wait, I will get your pouch of bones for you!" And he scampered off — fast, fast, faster.

It was a long, long way the rat had to go, but he didn't stop running day or night till he reached the brothers' village, and then his little legs ached for weariness. It was in the dusk of early morning that he came to the brothers' hut. The brothers were in there asleep. The rat climbed up the roof pole, where the pouch of bones hung by a cord. He gnawed through the cord, took the pouch of bones in his mouth, slid down the roof pole, and away with him.

But as he was going through the door with the pouch of bones dangling from his mouth, that pouch hit against the ground and rattled. The eldest brother woke. "Hey! Hey! Hey! Stop thief, stop!" The eldest brother was after him, running with all his might.

The eldest brother ran; the rat ran. Poor little rat: his legs were so tired, and the pouch of bones in his mouth was a heavy, awkward load. The eldest brother was catching up with him; he reached out and grabbed the rat by the tail; the rat turned and bit the eldest brother's hand; the pouch fell from the rat's mouth; the eldest brother reached out with his other hand and grabbed at the pouch. Ah ha! He will have it again! "I have it again, Mr. Rat! I have it again!"

Had he got it again? No, he hadn't! Down from the sky swept a hawk, the hawk that Jiri had once long ago caught in a snare and set free with his blessing. The hawk gave the eldest brother a peck on the nose that sent him sprawling. Then the hawk snatched up both pouch and rat and flew away with them to Jiri.

"Oh, my rat, oh, my hawk, how can I ever thank you?" Jiri took the pouch of bones and threw it on the ground. "I wish that my village comes back to me with all that it contains!"

No sooner said than done. There is his village again; there are the pretty, trickling springs and streams of water; there are the lowing cattle, the grain fields, the pasture fields, the decorated straw huts, the happy, smiling people. And there is Jiri's pretty, laughing wife, running to throw her arms round him.

But there also are Jiri's two brothers, with scowls in their hearts and false smirks on their faces.

"Jiri, we have done very wrong. Jiri, forgive us! Jiri, do not turn us out into the desert to die! Jiri, give us a home!"

And Jiri answered, "Yes, I will give you a home, but it shall not be my home, for your ways are not my ways."

Then he threw the pouch of bones on the ground and said, "I wish a village for my brothers, but let that village be far, far from here. And let there be a mark set on the ground between them and me: a mark they may not cross over."

And as he said, so it was done. The two brothers vanished from his sight, nor did he ever see them again.

So with his pretty, laughing wife, among his happy, smiling people, Jiri lived in great contentment. His friend the rat scampered about his hut and slept on his hearth. His friend the hawk hovered over his fields and slept on his roof. The pouch of bones Jiri hung from his door post that he might bow to it in gratitude as he went out and in. And sometimes, on quiet summer evenings, when Jiri sat in his doorway under the pouch of bones, the kindly ghost came there and talked with him.

The Bunyip

A tale from the Dreamtime, when the aborigines of Australia needed to fish in water
holes but lived in fear of what might be hiding in the dark waters, ready to attack from
the unknown depths.

✌

*I*n the beginning, when the world was made, that was
the Dreamtime. On the vast, sunbaked plains of Australia, the outback, stories of the Dreamtime are told
by the aborigines, the slender, black people who move
so quickly and lightly through that harsh land. At night,
around their campfires, they have told the stories.
Mothers have told them to their children, and the tribes
have danced them at their corroborees and sung them
at their singsongs for at least thirty thousand years.
"Why do you have to write your stories down?" the
aborigines ask the white people. "We carry our stories
in our heads."

They remember how Nagacork, an old man like
God, made the world, and how the dusty red deserts
were once full of forests and swamps where huge,
strange animals lived. They remember how all the animals and birds and snakes, and even the sun and moon
and stars, were once men and women, and they know

how they were changed. Even now, each aborigine tribe has a totem, a sign or symbol of the tribe, perhaps an animal or a bird. Some say that the aborigines can change into their totems and back again. And though some aborigines have left the outback and live among white people, they are still children of the Dreamtime. This is one of their stories.

One day, long, long ago, some young men left their camp to get food for their tribe. Bulloo, the youngest man, was not yet married. He was in love with a girl, but she had not promised to marry him. Before he left the camp, he said to her, "When we come back, I will bring you such a fine present that you will see I am the strongest and best hunter of our tribe." Then he said, "*Bo bo*," which means good-bye.

The sun was hot as the young men left the shelter of the caves in an outcrop of rock where the tribe lived, but as they traveled they ran races and competed in throwing their spears and boomerangs. Bulloo won every race. His spear went the farthest, and he threw his boomerang so skillfully that it always returned to him.

At last they reached a deep water hole surrounded by bulrushes. Some of the young men wanted to plait baskets and fill them with bulrush roots, which the tribe liked to eat. But Bulloo said, "Making baskets and pulling up roots is women's work. They can do that for themselves. Let us fish."

The others agreed. They made fishing lines from the

bark of the mimosa tree and found worms for bait. But Bulloo had different bait. In his dilly bag he had brought some raw meat for his dinner. From this he cut off a piece and baited his line with it.

For a long time the young men fished patiently without getting a single bite. The sun was sinking, and it seemed they would have to go home empty handed without even a basket of roots for the women and children.

Suddenly Bulloo's line disappeared under the water. Something very heavy was pulling so hard that he could barely keep his footing. He must have caught an enormous fish! He fought to hold his line, but he knew that he must either let go or be dragged into the water hole. Bulloo called for help, and the others came to pull with him, though they were trembling with fear of what they were going to see.

With one last tug they landed on the shore a strange creature, something like a huge snake, or a long-necked bird, or a demon calf, or a seal, but none of these. They looked at each other with horror, for though they had never seen such a thing, they had heard from their fathers and grandfathers about this monster — a bunyip, not full grown but still terrible, more feared by the people of the outback than any other monster.

As they stood motionless with fright, the bunyip cub gave a low wail. This was answered by another wail from the far side of the water hole. Then a much larger creature — the mother — rose from her underwater

home and came toward them, rage flashing in her horrible yellow eyes. She gnashed her fangs at the men who had her cub.

"Let it go! Let it go!" whispered the young men to one another. But Bulloo said that he had caught it and he was going to keep it. He had promised the girl he loved that he would bring back a fine present. They could not eat the bunyip cub, but children could play with it, he said. Flinging his spear at the mother, he threw the little bunyip onto his shoulders and set out for the camp while the mother roared in grief and pain. His friends followed him, hoping that all would be well.

By this time the plain was in shadow, but the young men ran toward home. They had escaped from the bunyip! Suddenly they heard a low rushing sound behind them and, looking back, saw that the water hole had risen out of its banks. The spot where they had landed the bunyip was flooded.

"What is happening?" they asked one another. "There is not a cloud in the sky, and even when it rains, the water hole has never overflowed like this!"

For an instant they watched, then turned and ran with all their might, Bulloo running faster than anyone else.

When he reached the high rocks that overlooked the plain, he turned to see if he was safe yet. Safe? Only the tops of trees showed over that oncoming sea, and they were fast disappearing. "Run faster!" he called to his friends. So on they sped, scarcely feeling the ground as they ran, till they flung themselves down before the caves where they had all been born.

The old men were sitting there, the children were playing, and the women chattering together, when the little bunyip fell into their midst, and they knew that something terrible was going to happen.

"The water! The water!" gasped Bulloo. And there it was, slowly but steadily mounting. Parents and children clung together, as if together they could drive back the flood, and Bulloo, who had caused all this catastrophe, cried, "Find higher trees!"

But as he spoke, something cold touched his feet, and he glanced down. Then with a shudder he saw that they were feet no longer but bird's claws. He looked at the girl he loved and beheld a great black bird standing at his side. He turned to his friends and saw instead a flock of awkward waddling creatures. He put up his hands to cover his face, but they were no longer hands, only the ends of wings. And when he tried to speak, a noise such as he had never heard before came from his throat, which had suddenly become long and slender. Already the water had risen to his waist, and he found himself sitting easily upon it, while its surface reflected back the image of a black swan, one among many.

So far as anyone knows, the black swans never again became people, but they were still different from other swans, for in the nighttime those who listened could hear them talk in a language that was certainly not swans' language. There were even sounds of laughing and talking, more like people than swans.

The bunyip cub was carried home by its mother, and after that the waters sank back to their own channels. The side of the water hole where the bunyip lives is always shunned by everyone, because nobody knows when she may suddenly put out her head and draw a victim into her mighty jaws. But people say that underneath the black waters she has a wonderful home such as mortals cannot imagine. Nobody has ever seen it. Some say that the black swans, who are awkward on land but graceful in the water, can turn themselves back into the graceful people of the Australian outback. But nobody knows for sure. Nobody has seen it happen.

And what became of Nagacork, the old man who made the world? He went on a long walkabout to see what had happened to all of the people and animals, birds, snakes and fish, the sun and moon and stars that he had created. This was his singsong as he traveled: "*Cha nallah, wirrit, burra burra, cubrimilla, cubrimilla.*" It meant, "You have all changed your shapes, but your spirits belong to me. I am going now, and you will never see me again, yet I will be watching over you. *Bo bo.* Good-bye."

Joe Magarac, Steel Man

The old steel mills of Pittsburgh may have become a thing of the past, but the ghosts of the great men who worked there still haunt the river valley, forever facing the flames of the open-hearth furnaces.

୧୬

Did you ever see Joe Magarac alive? No? Well, it's too late now, because he isn't alive anymore, not like you and me, that is. But you might still see his ghost, if you knew where to look, along the Monongahela River. You don't know where the Monongahela is? Then you don't live in western Pennsylvania, where the Pittsburgh steel mills used to stand all along the shores of the Monongahela.

You never saw a steel mill? Well, we can't all be that lucky. A hundred years ago the chimneys of the steel mills filled the sky with black, sooty smoke, because inside those mills were the open-hearth furnaces that burned night and day making steel. Barges brought loads of iron ore and coke and limestone and scrap metal down the Monongahela River to feed the hungry furnaces. At night, smoke and flame lit up the sky like fireworks.

In those days Pittsburgh was called the Steel City.

It was famous all over the world for making steel, and men from Poland and Yugoslavia, from Czechoslovakia and Hungary, came to Pittsburgh to work in the mills. Before long, they were all Americans. Joe Magarac came from Hungary. He was a real steel man and a real American, you bet. Seven feet tall.

Joe Magarac arrived in Pittsburgh at night. When he saw fire in the black sky, he got off the train and walked into the employment office of the first mill he could find.

"Where's the boss?" he said.

"I'm the boss in this office," said the employment manager. "Do you want a job?"

Joe nodded, so the boss said, "Write your name here."

Joe wrote on a paper, and the boss looked. "Joe Magarac. That's some name. In Hungary where I come from, *magarac* means donkey."

Joe smiled a big smile. "You from Hungary? Me, too. Magarac. Donkey. I work like a donkey. Never get tired."

"You don't speak much English," said the boss, writing on the paper.

"Only American, a little," said Joe. "But I'll learn."

"You married?" the boss asked.

"I got no time for a wife."

"Where do you live?"

"Nowhere yet. I'll get a room."

"What can you do?"

"Work, eat, sleep, work. You show me the work. Never mind eat and sleep. Give me a job."

"How's your health?"

"Good," said Joe. "I'm strong." He pounded on his chest, and the boss heard a sound like a hammer hitting steel.

"Come on then," said the boss. "I'll show you the furnaces. We need another man on Number Seven. Now here's how we make a heat of steel."

They went across the mill yard past mountains of scrap metal. Overhead, cranes with giant magnets were lifting loads of scrap and dumping the metal into rail cars that ran to the furnace doors. A machine with a finger ten feet long pushed the metal into the furnace, and the flames leapt up, white hot, to meet it. The glare from the flames was fierce. The boss gave Joe some smoked glasses and a shovel. He pointed to a pile of limestone.

"This limestone is to keep the furnace from melting," he said. "You get in line and shovel it against the front wall. You'll be third helper. Later you can learn to make back wall." Inside the furnace the metal bubbled and boiled. "Hot enough for you?" said the boss.

"Good," said Joe. "I like it fine. Like making candy."

The boss pointed to a big man, six feet tall. "That's Pete. He's second helper. Keep shoveling until he says to stop."

Joe shoveled. He shoveled all night long, six nights

a week, lining the walls of the furnace with limestone. He swung his shovel so well that before long he could make back wall. To make back wall, all the men on Number Seven formed a line and marched one after another like a team to the open furnace door. When Joe's turn came, he stared into the fire to place his throw. Then he flung his shovelful across the flames to the back wall, where it landed just right.

"Okay," Pete would say. "Now she can cook a while."

The first helper watched the cooking every few minutes through peepholes in the furnace doors. The fires burned hotter and hotter.

The steel might take ten hours to cook or twenty-four. After a few hours the first helper would scoop out a giant spoonful and pour it into a mold. "Like candy," said Joe.

When the metal cooled, the first helper broke it with a sledgehammer. Sometimes he would say, "Got to cook some more." Finally, after many tests, he would nod. "Looks good. Tap her out."

Below the furnace was a crane holding a mammoth ladle, so big it could hold enough candy to feed a thousand giants. Joe stood with other men on a platform above the ladle. They waited. Then — "*Yeow!*" At that signal from the first helper, the second helper poked a rod up a spout from the furnace. Out came the molten metal in a fiery, red, hissing, rumbling stream, flowing down the spout into the ladle. The first and second helpers staggered close to the ladle with bags of something heavy and poured it in. That sent the flames up to the roof, flashing around the men on the platform.

"What's that?" Joe asked the second helper.

"Manganese."

Joe shrugged his shoulders. "I don't know that language, but I'll learn."

"Manganese hardens steel," said the second helper. "Here come the ingot molds."

On tracks below the ladle, a train of cars was carrying molds the shape of candy bars seven feet high. Ingot men with metal rods stood on a platform above the molds. The crane operator swung the full ladle carefully over the first mold, and the ingot men used their rods to open a small hole like a faucet in the bottom of the ladle. When the mold was full, the men turned off the faucet and the second mold moved into place. After a while a whole row of ingots had been made and turned out of the molds like solid blocks of glowing fire.

"Easy!" said Joe, grinning from ear to ear. "Let me do that."

"You wait," said the second helper. "It's not so easy. If the handle sticks and the ladle keeps on pouring and it's all over the floor . . . You want to know how hot hell is? You wait and see when that stuff gets loose."

"I can turn any handle," Joe said. "I'm strong. *You* wait. You'll see."

And sure enough, when Joe Magarac got to be second helper and filled the molds, the handle on the ladle faucet never did get stuck. Joe did every kind of job in the steel mill, except the paperwork, and wherever he was, things went fine.

The worst job was getting inside the furnace to relay the brick lining. That had to be done between making heats, of course, but it was still hotter than the hinges of hell. You had to dig out the old bricks with a pickax and cement in new ones. You had to be hosed off every time you went in and came out, and even then your hair was singed and you got burns on your face and arms. Joe didn't mind relaying brick. He would grin and say, "Let me do it. I like it hot."

Then one day Joe didn't show up for work. Nobody knew just why he left. Some of the men said he had found a job in a bigger mill farther down the river. Business had started to slow down in Pittsburgh, and some said Joe had gone out to South Chicago, where business was booming. But there were other, strange explanations. One man said he had seen Joe sitting on the edge of a ladle stirring the boiling metal with one arm. Another man said he had seen that, too, and that Joe had climbed right into the ladle and sat there smiling and waving until he melted and disappeared. That would explain why they never saw Joe again, because anything or anyone that got into a ladle became part of the molten steel, so if that's what happened to Joe, he was turned into steel rails, or girders for a skyscraper or tools or nails, or whatever the mill was making at that time.

Stranger than Joe's sudden disappearance were the

things that kept on happening after he left. One day a little boy who liked to play hooky was hanging around the mill instead of going to school. He was carrying water for the men who were building a new furnace. They told him he ought to go home, but they let him stay because he kept the water bucket filled. About quitting time, he started to climb a long ladder that went all the way from the ground to the scaffolding over the furnace, about eighty feet up. Just for fun.

The boy was halfway up the ladder before anyone saw what he was doing. Then one of the men shouted for him to come down. But he just looked down and laughed and kept going, rung by rung, until he was about seventy feet above the ground. By this time there was a whole crowd of men at the foot of the ladder, all shouting, "Come down! Come down!" And once more he turned to look down and laugh. Suddenly he got sick and dizzy. He almost fainted. All he could do was to hang on, slumped against the ladder. If he fell, he would be killed.

Some of the men ran for another ladder. They telephoned the fire department for a net. Everyone was giving advice and screaming. Then a man appeared from somewhere. He was very big. He pushed through the crowd, took hold of the bottom of the ladder, and slowly lifted it until the ends rested against his thighs. Then he turned the ladder around so that it cleared the furnace and very gently brought it to the ground. When the boy was safe, everyone was busy getting him

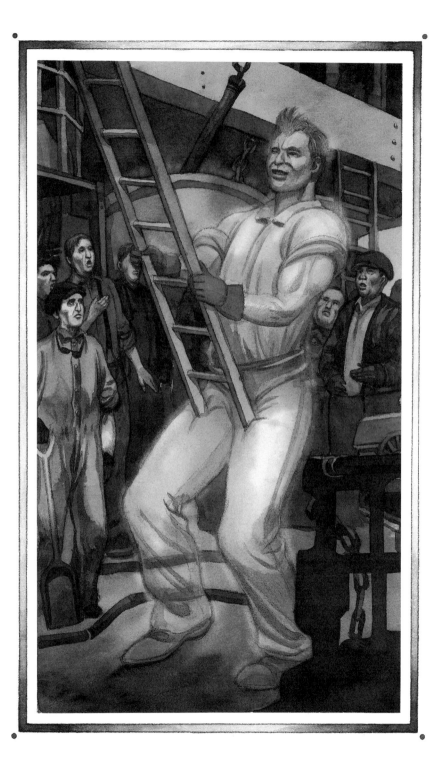

into an ambulance so the hospital could make sure he was all right. No one saw what happened to the big man, but afterward they said it must have been Joe Magarac. Nobody else could have handled that ladder the way he did. Or was it his ghost?

Another time there was an order for five hundred kegs of nails for a warehouse down in Memphis on the Mississippi River. The kegs went by rail and were pulled down to the loading wharf a mile away where they were reloaded on a barge. It wasn't hard or dangerous work like the work in the mill. But that day the river was swollen with spring floods and the barge was riding high in the water. The river was running fast and the mooring ropes were old. The barge tugged hard against them. Suddenly it began to rain cats and dogs. The men ran across the loading chute onto the barge to get under cover. They weighed enough to make the barge sway away from the wharf. Then the ropes broke. The barge couldn't be steered because the towing boat hadn't come yet. Well, there was the barge out of control on the river, gathering speed all the time, and about a hundred yards down the river was a stone bridge with close-set arches. The barge couldn't miss crashing into that bridge. The men were yelling and screaming, sure that they were going to be killed. But the next minute, the barge stopped and stood still. Then it started to move backward, back up the river against the current, until it got to the wharf. Some of the men jumped out and tied up the barge, but one of them looked out toward the middle of the river and swore he saw a man swimming out there. It was a giant of a man, and he turned his head and waved. When the other men looked, all they could see was a little mist and a lot of rain. So what do you make of that? It had to be Joe Magarac, didn't it? Or maybe his ghost.

And then there was the time when Number Seven furnace was ready to tap. The men were all in their places and the first splashes of molten steel struck the bottom of the ladle. But something was wrong with the flow. It seemed to be jammed up. The second helper poked about with his long rod, but the flow still didn't come right. It would start and stop.

When the ladle was about three-quarters full, it happened. The rear wall of the furnace split, and molten steel, white hot, came pouring out like Niagara Falls into the huge pot. And when the crane operator lifted the ladle to place it over the ingot molds, a crack started up near the rim. The crack widened as the ladle came nearer and nearer the men. In another second, tons of molten steel would have poured down on them. But that instant, one of the men grew to the size of a giant with huge shoulders and arms towering up above the fifty-ton ladle. He took hold of the edges of the crack and forced them together again. The men who had been shrieking with terror shouted for joy. But the giant was gone as fast as he had come. The ladle was moving along normally. They couldn't believe their eyes. All they knew was that Joe Magarac had saved them.

When they had to mend the lining of the broken back wall they wished he was there to do it. That job was hotter than the hinges of hell. "But Joe would do it and keep smiling," the men said. "He never minded the heat. Joe Magarac, the best steel man of us all. Come on, let's do it!"